death letter blues

m.a.elgazzar

ISBN 978-0-578-01115-8

Printed in the U.S. by Lulu.com

For Anna and Laila

"I'm bitter about being bitter"

death letter blues

Around 11:30 every morning, the sun creeps around the corner of the building I live in; intense rays spilling through the gaps in the blinds onto my sleeping eyes. My body shuffles in the folds of the blanket and my head turns on the pillow. Burying myself under the shade of an arm or turning towards the dark wall remains futile; there is no more sleep in my day. The worst is over. I'm awake. My legs jolt, pulling the blanket down past my knees. A rush comes over my body. I sit up.

elgazzar

The apartment stays messy with empty pizza boxes, ashtrays teeming with half-smoked cigarettes, and knocked over paper coffee cups. In the sink by the window there are three dishes and an empty pot for water sitting on the adjacent stove. The air is thick with dust, ash, and my own body heat. I must have sweat last night in my sleep. I peel away from the bed and wander towards the toilet.

The best piss of the day is the one you refuse to get up in the middle of the night to take and let loose in the morning. The moment's bliss interrupted by the abrasive clamor of the telephone; it resounded through the air. I was surprised to hear my apartment's phone ring; usually I received calls on my cell phone, a much gentler tone. The ringing stopped. I paused for the next set of bells. It didn't come. I focused back on my bladder. The phone screamed again: Murphy's Law. I flushed.

"Hello?"

"Ruiz? Ruiz, Bernard?" the woman's voice on the other end inquired.

"Who's speaking?" I needed information before I answered any questions.

"This is your Auntie GiGi," the voice announced, expecting some sort of reciprocal excitement.

2

"Who?" I let her down.

"Your Auntie GiGi! Don't you remember me? I know it's been a long time since we've seen each other. But..."

"Are we related? Do I know you?" We must've been kin since she called herself 'Auntie', but I don't remember anybody by that name. Really, I don't remember many people.

"Of course we're related! Your mother, rest her soul, was my good friend in school. We spent hours together each day, we sold lemona..."

"Good friends? So I don't really know you then." I had to make this conversation brief before she digressed into the rising cost of lemons and the obvious shame it is to have to pay one dollar for a cup of lemonade instead of the old twenty-five cents.

"Well, I met you once when you were young."

"So we've met. How did you get this number?" I was curious.

"A few years ago, before your mother passed on, she gave me a list of her important phone numbers. And your were on that list."

"Well, I know that you didn't call to chat," it was a short reply despite my pleasure in knowing that I was important to my mother.

"I remember you being witty and somewhat sharp-tongued," she chuckled, "even as a young boy."

Is it possible that we get to the point of this exchange? I'm bored with this. My eyes rolled and my breath sighed with her every passing word. I wasn't witty; I was just bored. GiGi's cheerfulness began to irritate me. To me, this cheerfulness was a profound insincerity. After all, how can a person be so happy to somebody they don't know? Was this a sign of discomfort? Or perhaps GiGi felt an obligation to be nice to me based on an outdated relationship with my mother, in which case it would still be insincere. "So what is it that you wanted?"

"Your mother was in distress before she married your father. She always hid her feelings with him for fear he would leave her. During this time, after not speaking with her for almost two years, she showed up unannounced at my doorstep. She asked me to harbor a chest and promised that she would return for it someday. She never did."

death letter blues

"So you want me to come by and pick up this box?" again, I tried to speed up this phone call.

"Not quite," she replied, "I thought there would be no harm in opening the chest. At first, it seemed like it was full of junk and random memorabilia. But when I began to look closely, there were letters, jewelery, and photos that must have signified this turbulent time. Clearly, while not to you or me, these items carried a lot of value to your mother. There was one letter in particular that was addressed to a man in Canada. Based on the postage and the numerous 'Return to Sender' stamps, it must have been important. I think that your mom really wanted to send this letter."

"Well, what does the letter contain?" I asked.

"I can't say. It's sealed," GiGi answered.

"So open it up and read it," I commanded, "no use in waiting around anymore. I don't think we're invading anyone's privacy."

"Oh! Heaven's No! I would never open up a sealed letter like this if it didn't belong to me!" GiGi was clear on her position, "Besides, it's a federal offense."

"No?" I was confused.

"No!" she confirmed.

"So now what?" I asked.

"So now you are going to deliver this letter," she declared.

There was a long pause. I attempted to piece together the different parts of the conversation so I could at least grasp the essence of our exchange. I refused to believe that it all came down to the last thing she demanded of me. She wanted me to deliver a letter to some place in Canada? And when was I supposed to do this? What did the letter say? Was this guy even alive? I had so many more questions but I just wanted to get off the phone.

"Why don't you deliver the letter?" Passing the buck is always easy.

"I'm old, dear. I can't make that kind of trip."

"Get somebody else to do it," I suggested.

"She was your mother," she came back.

I offered up another suggestion, "Just send it in the mail or by courier."

"Apparently, your mother tried sending it at least five or six times and it hasn't worked, so I don't think it'll work this time," she was prepared with some replies.

death letter blues

"What makes you think I'll be able to deliver this letter, the contents of which neither one of us are aware of, if the postal service can't? You know: Snow, Sleet, or Rain the mail must get through," I couldn't remember exactly what their motto was.

"You care," she confidently announced.

"No I don't," was waiting on the tip of my tongue and without hesitation it came.

"Yes, you do," she was convinced, "And besides, you've got nothing better to do."

She was officially bothering me at this point, "How do you know?"

"Because witty boys like you don't get good grades in school because they're too smart and bored in class with others they think are stupid and they never get the jobs they want because the idiots who got better grades went to college and took the jobs, so you don't really care about the work you do and don't mind leaving it. What is it? Are you a line cook? An errand boy? A landscape, ahem, artist?" Her blood was getting hot.

Again with the 'witty'. She was right about the work though.

"I don't fly," I began posing problems and obstacles.

"Why not?" she asked.

"I was born that way," simple enough, I thought.

"Take a bus."

"No money."

"I'll pay," she threw in her trump. I can't say that I was convinced by this offer, not that she wouldn't have paid, but it was no reason for me to travel.

"OK, fine."

"I'll drop the letter off in the morning," she rejoiced.

death letter blues

Rarely did guests enter the apartment's space. It was a container that held only my existence. Upon opening the front door, my body dissipated into the room. There, I strove for nothing, I didn't move forward. I made no progress. Something would interrupt this idle rest; something always did. Last night, I couldn't sleep because of it. The creeping sun didn't wake me today. It was something else, the sense of an outside intruder.

It seemed early in the morning when the sudden, firm rasp on the door began. My sleep was troubled, so my eyes opened easily and I was alert. Without hurrying, my feet pitter-pattered below my body, bringing me towards the entrance. My subtle turn of the handle became a swift push from a foreign force. My muscles clenched and I became guarded.

"Hello Ruiz," a round woman in her sixties wrestled with the door. Her hair was short, curly, and clearly dyed wine red. Her calf-length beige skirt revealed a comfortable but elegant leather shoe. She wore turquoise jewelery over a jet-black mock turtleneck. It was GiGi; I could tell from her voice. Then I remembered that she was to drop off the letter. And finally, as clear as it may have been to someone else, I understood why my sleep was disturbed. She quickly out maneuvered the piles of refuse and furniture scattered throughout the apartment. Her hands conservatively remained close to her body; I could tell she was thinking about rats, insects, germs, viruses, and other progressively smaller and potentially infectious and lethal microorganisms when she hesitated to touch anything. I knew the space was messy, but I never thought I could get sick just existing there. And I never did ail. She probably wondered whether or not my mother raised me to clean up.

death letter blues

"I would offer you a chair, but I'm convinced you won't sit. So where's this mythical letter?"

"I better not," she agreed. GiGi continued to examine the kitchen and then the bathroom as she produced two compact packages from her burgundy purse.

The two packages consisted of two orange mailing envelopes, folded over and bound with a rubber band. One was thicker than the other. I tore through the adhesion on the thinner of the two envelopes and pulled out yet another envelope. For a moment, I thought this was a game or perhaps a series of old Russian Matryoshka dolls. This was an even smaller note, faded and dusty with postage, post office marks, and the many 'Return to Sender' stamps that GiGi mentioned yesterday on the phone. Reaching for the second, thicker envelope, GiGi announced that it was the money she promised. I pulled out the stack of bills and riffled through what seemed to be about one or two thousand dollars.

"You are aware that I could just take these two envelopes and promise that I will deliver, but just pocket the cash and burn the letter?" I inquired of GiGi.

elgazzar

"I know that you won't. You're a good boy. And besides, I know people that'll ensure you either deliver or at least pay me back," GiGi assured me of her status.

"Like I said before, you could just have one of your henchmen take the letter then," I came back with another recycled comment.

"They're only dependable in certain matters," GiGi spoke with an ominousness of wealth, connection, and ability to make dangerous things happen. It made me a bit nervous. For a while I thought about how my mother had come to know this woman and how much this woman must've changed since first meeting mother. I wondered if mother had anything to do with GiGi's new direction. Of course, I would never ask this woman the details of her work or her social life. Put simply: it was scary for me to be around GiGi. She ignited an unexpected panic that rang deep inside me.

"Don't let your mother down," GiGi included as she sealed her purse, dusted off her hands and headed for the front door. She hesitated for a moment, turned back, and in a highly uncomfortable fashion approached me with puckered lips. I stood still; I dared not move a muscle. She left lipstick traces on my left cheek as she softly patted my right. Confidently, she turned again and strutted towards the door and down the hallway. My apartment was cleansed by the building's hallway draft. I hoped to catch the closing door before it slammed.

Thinking about all the changes that had just transpired in the last few hours, I stood silent and motionless in the middle of my apartment. I quickly concluded that this was all an unnecessary disturbance and the sooner I delivered, the sooner I could resume my routines. It had been at least two and half years since I last traveled. Generally, I appreciated the safety and predictability of the surrounding city blocks. Venturing much further than that caused a panic in me. I've tried to move farther, but there was nothing I could do to prevent these panics from occurring. There were no other ways to think about traveling other than it was an uncomfortable process that took me farther and farther from where I wanted to be. That's all it was to me. And now, GiGi and her red-dyed hair forced me to once again move beyond the limits of what I find to be adequate and sufficient. I reviewed the conversations and re-ran the reasoning that she used to get me to do what she wanted. How was it that she talked me into this? Things weren't making much sense. We were past the point of rebellion and she came in with one objective, the result of which was guaranteed on my part. She knew, somehow, that I would do exactly what she asked; I would do exactly what she demanded.

My body remained still for a few more moments, trying to understand the series of incomprehensible events that had just taken place. I reached into my pockets and felt the letter as well as the money. The letter came out of my pocket and threw itself on the round coffee table next to my couch. It taunted me. I stared at it for no less than fifteen minutes. It was staring back through its outer, faded, aged shell. The harder we gazed at one another, incapable of interacting in any genuine way, the harder it pulsated. The apartment, the couch, the ambient noise from the street, and even the coffee table faded in the shadow of the letter's throbbing self. We sat in still silence for several moments; externally, we ignored each other's inquisitive but passive natures, internally, we agonized for each other. After all, we gave each other something to do. My throat itched. I got up for a glass of water. I paused, and then thought about offering my guest a glass as well. I chuckled. I was getting ahead of myself.

My head began to entertain ideas of this upcoming trip. What would I pack? What would I pack it all in? How would I prepare for this journey? Were there people I was supposed to notify of my travels? I was overwhelmed. I lay on the couch. Many more questions flooded my thoughts. I didn't want to have any of them; I didn't even want to think. The first few hours of the day were exhausting: sleeplessness, the knocking at the door, entertaining GiGi's idiosyncratic behavior, and of course the letter that occupied my space like a living, breathing tenant.

Several hours later, I awoke on the couch. The sun was still up. It wasn't late. My eyes immediately turned towards the letter on the coffee table as though it were calling my name, 'Ruiz, Ruiz!' What mystery did the pages tucked away in the envelope carry? What was this message that couldn't get through? Did the address still exist? I didn't understand. And while my curiosity spun endless circles, deep inside I think ignorance of the contents would serve me better. Surely if I knew what message was encrypted in the folds of the letter, there would exist no chance of my delivering it. I brainstormed the possibilities: overly romanticized and completely unrealistic love yearning for actualization in a world that simply doesn't care, an oft-too requested payment on services long past rendered, or perhaps an over-due apology for a slightly offensive comment made to a hypersensitive and hormonal personage. A battle raged between my desire to open the letter and a test of whether my hypotheses were correct on the one hand with the true apathy that existed inside of me. There was no question about the inevitably victorious apathy; in other words, I didn't care enough to consider any other possibilities. There was an inkling inside me that still burned with curiosity and I had to admit at some point that my lack of concern for the contents of the envelope was just a rationalization. I had to convince myself that I wasn't scared to know what was inside. There was something inside of me that made me afraid. I lay back down on the couch.

Police lights and ambulance sirens woke me up in the middle of the night. I peered out the window for a few moments surveying the commotion. Several young Black men were being questioned by uniformed officers under the awning of a nearby building. From where I stood, I could tell that none of the interviewees were interested in this conversation. Two of the men had their arms folded in front of their chests while the third scratched his head and repeatedly checked his watch. I could understand their distaste for the police. Otherwise, the situation could have ranged from a street killing to a burning building. I couldn't really tell. My mouth was dry and I longed for water.   The kitchen faucet dripped.   I put a glass underneath, turned the handle, and poured the stream into my gullet. I set the glass down and returned to the couch. Reaching for the pack of cigarettes, I stopped at the letter. I huffed while it reminded me of its presence. If only the cigarettes were in a different place, a different room, the other side of the table. After lighting up, I threw the lighter on the table and issued a sprawling cloud of smoke into the room.   I picked up the letter and attempted to make out the address, shrouded in red stamps, faded ink, and oily fingerprints. Some of the letters were faded:

Michcl Ril crg

161 Ruc dc Varemes

Mcnlrcal, QC HZT

Ccnc la

For several moments I believed the addressee as well as the address were Norwegian.   Pieces of letters were faded, some were missing completely.   I couldn't decipher the fives from the sixes and neither of those from the eights. I was going to Canada and I guess, specifically, Quebec. Whatever. The letter reoccupied its rightful territory on the coffee table, this time several feet from the cigarettes and the ashtray.

elgazzar

The couch prodded springs into my back; the soreness moved from lower back to upper back and then to my neck. I was tired. The bed didn't sound appealing strictly based on the number of footsteps I would have to endure to get there. I was too lazy to be lazy. I was too comfortable to get comfortable. Still, I could not sleep. I lit another cigarette to forget my fatigue. The nicotine coursing through my blood did not relieve my restless nature. Still, I was wide-awake and searched in terror for some entertainment. I fidgeted with a coin through my fingers. I set goals for the coin: flip over the tops of my knuckles then land in my palm and begin again. I would count the number of times the coin would flawlessly master the obstacles course of short, stubby fingers. It was an uncoordinated coin. The twenty-five cent piece navigated the hand circuit exactly zero times. The coin's copper-nickel clumsiness began to frustrate me. It whirled itself across the room and resonated against the hardwood floor upon death-defying crash landing. "Stupid quarter," I thought to myself, "it doesn't even know how to soften its touchdown." I would always want to be able to try one more time instead of going for broke with no possibilities of parole. The commotion on the street quickly subsided and it became silent with the exception of an occasional whir of a passing automobile.

Turning back to the coffee table in aspiration of finding more entertaining what-to-do-when-you-can't-sleep-activities, the dusty letter again signaled me with a flare. My eyes rolled back into my rotating head, hoping it would understand my disappointment. My company annoyed me; it demanded my attention at every possible moment; it caused an impairment in my ability to focus and concentrate on anything and everything that I really didn't feel like thinking about but preferred to its god-forsaken existence. In an agitated hurry, my body lunged towards the letter. I found the crumpled document and money in my hands. Another rush came over my body. My body temperature flashed hot then I exhaled. Looking down, I see the packages sitting at the bottom of a garbage bin. I offered my best sneering grin, lifted my eyebrows and returned to the couch. This is my space. No trespasser can impede my inevitable demise on this or that sofa. I will do without the unwelcome hindrances of the outside world.

The resounding tin of my brass cigarette lighter pleased me as I inhaled a few more puffs off a new cigarette. I repeated the gesture with my lighter for the same sound and, hence, the same pleasure. It faded quickly when I realized the clock on the wall read 3:42. Unbelievable! This letter so far caused in me a highly unsettling feeling; not to mention it will lead to numerous conversations I'll have with people I don't know. My face rested in my open palms. I was comfortable there. It was dark.

At that moment the cogs in my mind began to spin. I thought at length about the details of what GiGi really asked of me: being away from home, at least my apartment, for a long time and interact somehow with the external world until I returned. It hadn't fully dawned on me that I had agreed to all of this as well. Besides the haziness of sleepless morning grog, I was sober and it seemed like a dream to me. Over and over again visions of the previous day's events ran circles. At what point was I convinced? Was I ever convinced? Did I even agree? In a disbelieving anguish I turned to the coffee table and reached in my pockets for the evidence of this entire exchange. For a fraction of a second I was relieved at not being able to find the folded pieces of paper that represented a reality I was not too familiar with. Then I remembered; retracing my footsteps to the garbage can, a rush of defeat immersed me. With my disappointment, I gazed frantically at the letter and its cohort, the money. Then they looked at me with a sneering grin. Never did I laugh last.

Although this lifeless creature had defeated me, I didn't agonize. In fact, there was a certain peace that subsumed me. I felt calm. I fell asleep.

elgazzar

death letter blues

Again, I awoke before the sun. Would this become a habit for me? The best thing I could do would be to hope for long sleep. Slowly, I got out of bed and began to dress myself. There weren't many options in my closet or on my floor. Canvas cargo pants, white t-shirts, a thick military style over shirt, and simple, strong hiking boots were my staple dress. After my clothes, I pulled out a large canvas duffel and perused the apartment for the necessary garments. Nothing was clean and nothing seemed essential besides what I had already worn. I thought about extra socks or perhaps extra underwear, but I figured that obtaining new garb or washing the ones I was already wearing was sufficient. I looked around a bit more trying to find important and useful items. I picked up my cigarettes and refilled my brass lighter. The letter somehow found its way to my chest pocket. The money was split up: five hundred in my wallet and another five hundred in my pocket. The remaining thousand dollars were carefully rolled up and tucked into my boot. I remember my mother, the person who really got me involved in all this, telling me that splitting up money is not only smart for all the times that one could potentially get robbed, but also good for saving, as long as I forgot where I stashed it. Of course, I always knew exactly where my money was: one-hundred dollars in tens and twenties in the coffee can on the bookshelf, fifty-seven dollars on page fifty-seven of Descartes' "Meditations", two-hundred dollars in a shoe-box underneath my bed. I collected all the funds and distributed them on my person.

Naturally, at this point before any journey, I sighed. I walked towards the exit of my apartment and looked back at the messy space. For a moment I thought about cleaning the flat before leaving, but it was a fleeting hesitation and a quick decision: of course not. I walked out the door, slipped the key in the lock, and bolted the door. Down the hallway, the elevator was waiting. Slowly, I approached the shaft as the door began to close. It shut right before I got there. I pressed the call button and waited. The elevator lights did not move from floor to floor. I figured that passengers were loading and unloading on the different levels. I waited. I waited. I pressed the call button several more times frantically and began to think that this was all really a bad idea. I should just turn back and go home; it's only thirty-something steps away to my front door. The call button was lit and my pressing it would not speed up the elevator. I pressed it a few more times anyway, hovering around the closed elevator doors until a sign arrived: some sort of paranormal intervention that actually failed to comply with the rules of nature. No sign. The stairs were only a few strides away. There was no thinking about it; a charge inside my body propelled me down the urban mountain of concrete steps and stainless steel railings. After one flight, the clamor of the arriving elevator echoed through the halls. It was an easy sound to ignore once my muscles descended in their own rhythm. It was only three stories before the bright light of the street

elgazzar

was contrast with the tunnel of dark blue walls. My feet led me into the ocean of sunbeams.

death letter blues

The city streets were bustling with passing cars, buses, trams, and pedestrians. Everyone seemed to be in a rush. This was my first glimpse of the cityscape for days. The bright sunshine bounced off the windshields and seeped into the backs of my retinas. My arms shaded my eyes until my dilated pupils adjusted to the glaring beams. A steaming haze rose from the dark asphalt and immediately soaked into my boots. Already I became annoyed with the discomfort and once again I questioned my non-existent motives for traveling. Shrugging my

27

shoulders I began to move in the direction of the bus station.

I weaved in and out of people, their pets, and traffic for about nine blocks. An over-sized mesh net of individuals passed all around me; I slipped through the spaces. I didn't pay much attention to the passersby even though direct eye contact was made with many of them. Occasionally we would graze shoulders moving in opposite directions. Otherwise, I would seldom acknowledge their passing existence. Only if some culprit attempts to occupy the same time and space as me do I really care to bother myself with others.

Soon I arrived at Celine's Coffee Shop. The convenience of purchasing a ready-made cup of coffee coupled with a caffeine addiction exceeded the challenge of overcoming my distaste for public appearances. I asked for my coffee and stood waiting. It dawned on me that in the midst of a passing life, I must've spent hours on end just waiting for things to happen. Of course, nothing ever did. The attractive girl behind the bar haphazardly deposited my order on the counter and knocked over several hot beverages, including mine.

death letter blues

"Sir," she pouted, "have a seat and I'll bring your order out to you." My patience was challenged once more and I would have to wait. I turned to find a seat. She must have been exhausted from preparing the world's variety of drinks for all the upper class, pretentious art types who require exotic java beverages not because of their lethargy, but because their lavish lifestyles demanded servicing. The pink-collar service industry at this point was created to aid the disabled bourgeoisie in its public display of pampering. There was a seat at a table at the end of a long and oddly shaped room. I fell onto an intolerably stiff wooden chair. My body wriggled until it found a somewhat bearable position. My legs crossed and my elbow on the table, I awaited the arrival of the coveted injection of caffeine. A bit of an uproar ensued near the bar. Some lady became unsettled when the overworked barista delayed in taking her request. I settled into the idea that I would wait a few moments longer than anticipated while the workers shuffled to quell the commotion. Around the room, customers sat in groups waving their hands and carefully sipping their steaming libations, sharing with each other the events of last night's gallery opening and upcoming philanthropic ventures. At some points a shrilling outburst of giggles would accompany the kinesthetic story telling.

elgazzar

Others in the café perused the post-modern mess of art hanging on the walls, critiquing the work of people they didn't know with words they didn't understand. These conversations triggered an ambiance of pseudo-intellect and the sort of escapism that can only be expressed by beings who are far removed from themselves. Where was my coffee? I was ready to leave. I sat up in my chair. The girl working behind the register caught my eye and hustled. It seems she had forgotten. If only I didn't have to think about the atmosphere or the people in the shop. She shuffled over to my table, apologizing for the delay, explaining the commotion in front. I blinked my eyes and my jaw dropped in disbelief. This cute girl became very annoying and very unattractive very quickly. She spoke endlessly without any other aim than to mask her nervousness. Her speech was shrouded with and then's and like's.

"Just stop!" I blurted out. My mouth acted on its own accord and in a rare show of compassion, I softened the edges with, "Don't worry about it." With chagrin, she silenced herself, slightly dropped her shoulders, and indignantly turned towards her post. Without any thought, I stood up and walked out the back door.

death letter blues

The bus station was only a few blocks away. It was an over-sized monstrosity of poured concrete: modernism's wet dream. The architectural nightmare dominated the entirety of one whole city block, partially tucked underneath the highway overpass. It was flanked by large parking lots filled with the type of cars that only people who ride the bus would own. Of course, I didn't have a car. When GiGi first handed the money over, I did have a passing thought of buying an old beater, but alas, the torture of negotiating the sale price of an outdated vehicle surpassed the comfort of driving cross-country. The buses would enter one side of the building and exit on the other. Passengers would board and disembark somewhere inside the building's intricate labyrinth of asphalt ramps and tunnels. I traversed the large parking lot and stood at the mouth of the building.

Once I stepped inside the bus station, all sunlight evaporated into florescent overhead buzzing. There wasn't a single window inside the depot. An arctic gust took hold of me and raised hairs on the back of my neck. Summer time air conditioners always annoyed me because of the devices' penchants for causing malaise due to the extreme temperature and humidity swings between being outside and walking into almost any building. I popped the collar on my over-shirt to warm my neck. Inside the front door there was a kiosk selling snacks, a couple of soda machines, the grab-the-fuzzy-toy-with-the-totally-loose-claw-that-only-likes-to-eat-up-quarters game, and stairwells. Looking down the long corridor, people were lined up at their respective gates, waiting to board the buses tightly parked on the other side of the doors. Five ticket windows were located at the end of the long, spacious hallway; I made my way through the travelers and approached the booths.

"I need a ticket to," I fumbled through my pockets attempting to locate the letter.

"Sir?" The overflowing woman behind the glass began to speak, "Where do you want to go?" She spoke with a thick southern twang and some indignant undertones.

"Hang on just one second," I continued to search my clothing.

"Sir, please step away from the window while you find whatever it is you're looking for and don't block the line."

I turned and faced where people would normally be lined up. There was nobody there. I returned to the woman with a is-there-really-something-wrong-with-you-or-are-you-just-acting-like- that-on-purpose-look on my face. My jaw was dropped and I thought about how weird this all was. Couldn't she see that there was nobody behind me?

"Sir! Move!" She began to raise her voice and I sensed some animosity there. I stayed quiet. My silence wasn't an attempt to avert any potentially hostile situations. Her demeanor stirred a bit of fear in me. I was quiet because I was scared of her. Seated, she pushed her chair from under the desk littered with ticket stubs, receipts, and loose change. Immediately, I took a giant stride backward, oddly balanced with my hands in my pockets. Finally, I found the addressed letter.

By this time the woman behind the inch-thick glass was standing, hands on hips, daring me to return to her window.

"It's here!" I shouted from far, pointing to the letter waving in my other hand.

She raised one of her eyebrows.

"Where to?" She asked in a flabbergasted and somewhat defeated way.

"I found the address," my report fell on deaf ears.

"Where to?!" She cried.

"Montreal."

"Which one?" She examined me.

'Which one?' I thought to myself, 'which one?' If there were another Montreal, why would anyone go there? I couldn't believe she asked me that.

"How many are there?" I retorted with an arrogant air, "Montreal!"

"Montreal, eh?" She clarified in an ominous calm.

"Yeah! Montreal!" I couldn't help myself.

The round woman shook her double chin at me and honed in on her computer. Some screechy sounds emanated from the machine and eventually it produced a ticket.

"Eighty-five dollars, sir."

My hand dipped deep into my pocket and reluctantly forked over five twenty dollar bills. She produced some change for me and whipped the ticket through the window.

"It's leaving from gate seventeen in about three hours," She concluded our business and smiled. There must have been some sort of camera or microphone recording our conversation for training purposes. Her slight yet insincere change in attitude could easily be chalked up to job security. She kept the non-existent queue moving; when I began to get loud, she revoked her hostility; and rapidly created a worthy little piece of post-consumer paper that read 'Montreal' on it. I scooped up the documentation of rendered services and proceeded towards the bus station café. This old lady drained me of a sort of patience that I certainly was not born with and a cup of coffee sounded like a heaven send.

Stepping up to the trendy café counter, I remembered the long wait at the previous coffee shop. Secretly, I prayed to something greater than me to speed up whatever silly incident would surely occur.

"Just a cup of coffee please," I respectfully requested as I reached for some change.

"Would you like biscotti with that?" The bearded man behind the counter asked with an effeminate voice, waving his limp-wristed paw at the vacuum-sealed assortment of cookies.

"No, thank you."

"Well, could I interest you in a scone or some other snack?" He pushed a bit more as he carefully placed the coffee on the counter.

"No," my voice became slightly firmer and I eyeballed the man.

"How 'bout a..."

"NO! I only want this coffee. If I wanted something else, don't you think I would've asked for it?"

"No need for that, sir. Sometimes customers forget about our delicious snacks and it's my job to remind you know of them in case you have a taste for a little extra something with your coffee," he argued as he rubbed his receding hairline as if to push the absent bangs out of his face. I threw a couple of crumpled bills on the clearing of the counter and remained silent. At least this guy didn't spill the steaming beverage.

My body propelled me, as if by instinct, to the main doors of the bus station where I immediately lit a cigarette. The sickness that overcame me as I dealt with the various characters instantly evaporated as I inhaled this rocket of a coffin nail. Smoking often helped me sufficiently deal with other people. Sometimes, I would be trapped in conversation by the small groups crowded around an ashtray; their commiseration always began with complaints of their decade-long banishment from the indoors. A strange and unspoken solidarity always consumed these groups of nicotine-dependent outsiders. In unison, they often exhaled in the faces of passing snob-nosed uppity types, as if to say, 'You're the reason I'm out here in this stifling heat, you fucking intolerant fascists.' And when the trendy high-steppers vanished into their disgust, either around the corner of a building or into an entrance, the cast aways would inhale in silence and exhale in a multitude of chuckles and snickers. Their unparalleled revolutionary spirits triumphantly demoralized the health nuts, who still enjoy the undeterred flow of chlorofluorocarbon refrigerants cooling the indoor breeze. I dropped my cigarette, deadened it with the sole of my boot, and escaped back into the building before I was recruited into the vanguard of this blossoming rebellion against popular culture. Admittedly, my shame in being associated with these nonmembers paled in comparison to my lust for smoking. Certain sacrifices must be made for existing this way.

I found an empty chair in a row in front of my gate. I plopped onto the seat and looked up at the clock. More waiting. Two hours and a half of waiting to be precise.

37

elgazzar

The second hand on the clock slogged ahead at an eerily down-tempo pace. Looking around at fathers spanking their children, mothers engaged in uphill battles against resolute bus drivers, and couples holding on to each other as if for the last time, I couldn't help but think how people grasped on to their fleeting dreams for success as if real. The futility of their endeavors made me giggle. Were they not aware of their own death? So many of them confronted their inevitable fates with an undying determination to avoid it. Really, there are only two ways to deal with death: not bother to try anything or live today as if it were the last. I choose the former. Who needs an explanation? Who is wondering what the point of that is? It begs the question: there is no point to it. There is no need to try and create something out of nothing: A bunch of people drowning in the sludge of life that only exists in their minds, grasping their last breaths and perchance, praying for God's ark to sail by and rescue them from their inescapable futures.

The chatter, footsteps, and PA announcements echoing throughout the bus station halls created a somewhat peaceful and relaxing lull. The buzzing of mercury and argon in the long florescent tubes overhead, however, annoyed me. The ceiling installations designed to

death letter blues

light the place made such intolerable noises that the peaceful lull of chatter eventually became overrun with electrodes and photons. The noise that invaded my ears prevented me from dozing off. My wait would only conclude with wakefulness. I rubbed my eyes and continued to look around the room. The clock on the wall was my only reference as to how long I had actually been sitting here; there was really no way to know. Officially, I was bored.

elgazzar

death letter blues

"**P**assengers to Montreal, please proceed to gate seventeen," announced the articulate woman on the other side of the speaker system. "Passengers to Montreal."

As my legs stretched beneath me, lifting me to my feet, I straightened out my shirt and dusted off my pants. The gate was less than thirty feet away from where I was seated and yet, by the time I arrived at the counter, at least fifteen people had managed to create a small crowd hugging the exit. I remained at a distance as not to be bothered by any of their limbs. In a few hours I will long desperately for the fresh, cool, flowing air inside the bus station so I may as well enjoy it now by not breathing in the toxic body heat condensing in their armpits. I approached the bus driver before he disappeared into the masses.

"How long 'til we leave?" I asked.

"Oh, I say at least another thirty-five to forty minutes," he replied pushing his way through the exterior of the pack.

"So why did she have us come to the gate now?" I begged in confusion.

"Bags, luggage, babies, you know. It takes them a while."

"I'll be back in fifteen," I headed for another smoke.

When I got out to the front of the building, the crowd of smoking outcasts had dispersed. Finally, I had some time to myself to enjoy my cigarette. One of my hands robotically motioned back and forth, bringing my smoke to and from my gaping lips. The other hand reached deep into my pocket. My fingers ran along one of the edges of the folded letter and then I was reminded of the company I was in. I was reminded of the guest in my pocket; the purpose of my trip. It was the purpose of me. I exhaled. I dropped the butt and turned towards the bus. It was not the relaxing time alone that I had anticipated. My torso moved ahead with the help of its legs, charging through the gust of cold that welcomed me at the entrance, past the crying children pleading to their parents for quarters for the gum ball machines, beyond the Nazi double chins keeping the ticket line moving, and right into the crowd that slowly boarded the bus.

Every human creature getting on the bus asked a question as they passed the driver who patiently collected the tickets. He replied with quick 'yes', 'no', and 'I don't know' responses. There aren't many questions that can't be answered with those responses. I felt the driver was either an experienced man of life or at least an avid graduate of psychology. He was doing no more than simply penetrating the cold harshness of this world by meeting peoples' needs for security. As I observed his ill-fitting navy colored uniform stretching and shrinking to form his simple movements, he continued to provide attention and safety to so many of the control-addicts who wished they were driving. In an otherwise lonely and distant reality, this modest man aimlessly reached his hand; perhaps for the momentary contentment of not having to toil forward on his own. After all, he drove a bus full of passengers across the country and beyond. Why else would he choose this line of work? Perpetually lonely at the helm of this human freight, yet simultaneously, he is constantly surrounded by the passing relationships of needy travelers. I nodded to him and he to me as we exchanged small pieces of computer printouts that notarized our alliance if only for a given distance.

The aisle of the motor coach was flanked by two columns of seats on either side: one window seat and one aisle seat. All sorts of people were on the bus, although hard pressed to find a white man, unless, of course, he had a thick Russian accent. Weelkom doo Amereeka I would say to him as I chuckled. So many people brought home cooked meals along. There was no on-road service here; no ill-fitting and snug uniforms hugging the hips and pleasant breasts of entrepreneurial stewardesses selling sexuality from their carts as they strutted up and down the aisle. A lavatory was located at the back of the bus. When I was younger the optimal choice was, of course, the window. The sight of passing cars, trees, and signs blended into a mixture of color and shade that entertained me during the passage. These days, it made no difference where I sat. My ticket read '15-A'; a window seat. I slalomed around the groups of people forcing their enormous K-Mart plastic shopping bags stuffed with hand-me-down clothes into the limited overhead spaces. There it was, seat 15-A, wedged between a curtain rod with an emergency latch and a fairly burly fellow who was completely covered in a layer of hair.

"That's me, in there," I pointed to the empty chair. The hairy man looked at me through the breaks in his eyebrows, looked at the vacant seat, and then back at me. He clumsily pried himself out of the snug recliner and into the crowded aisle, causing a small but noticeable disturbance in our section of the bus. I swung into position and dropped myself on the cushion and looked back at the woolly fellow to express my satisfaction with how I had settled myself.

"I'm Joe," he announced with an outstretched paw.

"Ruiz," impulsively, I shook his hand.

"Where are you off to?" he inquired.

"Montréal."

"Hmm. I've never been," he thought out loud as I silently nodded with raised eyebrows to somehow signal a lack of interest.

"I'm on my way to Knoxville. To see some family," he volunteered without noticing my uncomfortable attempt at non-verbal communication. I nodded again without making any eye contact. The fuzzy beast of a man named 'Joe' wiggled his mitt onto the armrest dividing our seats. Some inexplicable prompt flashed in my mind, indicating that this movable piece of plastic separating me from this woolly mammoth with logs for arms would turn into hotly contested territory. Often, the unspoken war of elbows, ebbing and flowing onto this side or that, would result in a demilitarized green zone where trespassers would most certainly be shot. I've fought these very battles in movie theaters and waiting rooms but never in airline cabins at 35,000 feet, although I imagine the dynamics are very similar. I shifted my body to lean on the window and repositioned my other arm to serve as a makeshift pillow. In due time, my limbs would fall asleep beneath me triggering total numbness in stillness and within seconds of movement, outright spicular discomfort. At some point in our journey next to each other, Joe might wake from a nap to find me therapeutically rubbing my tingling appendage on his big, fleece belly for solace. I would simply look at him and say, 'My arm fell asleep,' and continue to knead my arm into his paunch.

My head rested on the window as I watched the people load their baggage in the cargo area and then scramble to find their seats. Whistles and hisses accompanied the suspension changes as the engine revved and pulled the bus from the gate. Immediately, I began to doze.

"Want a cookie?" asked fuzzy Joe.

"No thank you."

"They're good cookies. I couldn't find them anywhere so I ordered them on-line and I made sure they arrived before I left," the woolly man continued.

"No, really," I didn't want any cookies and I wasn't hungry.

"I insist!' he pushed. I took one of his cookies and held it in my hand so as to end the discussion.

"Well?" Joe asked.

"Well what?" I replied.

"Aren't you gonna eat it?"

"Nah. I'm saving it for later. Is that alright?"

"I have plenty more, so you can eat it now," He instructed me.

"But I'm not hungry for it now."

"Then why did you take it?"

47

"Why did I take it? Because you practically forced me to take it."

"I did no such thing."

"I refused the first several times you offered but you kept offering. I just wanted you to shut up," that was my first mistake. He snatched the cookie out of my closed hand, broke it in half in the process, leaving crumbs all over me. I dusted off my pants towards him and he huffed at me through his nose. And that's when I noticed that his hairiness was also endemic to his nose: long stringy vines outstretched for dust and odor, scaring little kids, and creating squirminess for anyone who bothered to get close enough to notice. It was silly of me to be rude to this hulking man. After all, any need I had on this bus would first be approved by him. He was my gatekeeper. He stood between the lavatory and me. He stood between freedom and me.

death letter blues

"Fifteen minute break!" yelled the bus driver. I awoke from a light doze and looked out the window. We were at a rest area with bathrooms and a few vending machines. I jumped up and tried to squeeze my way past the sleeping bear. Unfortunately, he woke up.

"Hey!" He screamed at me disapprovingly.

"Let me out," I plead.

"Why?"

elgazzar

"What difference does it make to you?" I tried to push through but he just kept getting in my way, bloating himself to fill in the empty spaces above and below the passage. I didn't realize this was Joe's way of arising from slumber. He was a crab. I thought I was bad in the mornings. "Just move."

Grizzly Joe finally got up and started towards the exit. It looked as though he was shedding like a cat when I observed his seat. There was also a sweat mark. I gagged. I was anxiously bouncing up and down behind him waiting to get off. Every step he took was slower than the first. And when he waddled down the steep bus steps, eventually descending off the bus completely, a hemorrhage of fresh air circulated into my nostrils and filled the bus, waking me in the process. It was a true dialysis of freshness. I preferred the burning scent of tar and nicotine.

My parched throat led me to the vending machines filled with cold beverages and three-month old twinkies, in other words, fresh snacks. I debated with myself for what seemed like fifteen minutes whether or not to purchase a drink that would only lead to another confrontation with fat Joe on my way to the lavatory to empty my bladder. I caved in and bought a soda anyway. The cool fizz rushed down my gullet. I turned to the bus, lit another smoke, inhaled it, and boarded.

Bigfoot was already sound asleep on the bus when I got to the fifteenth row. I looked around in case there was another empty seat. There were none. I carefully tiptoed past the sleeping beast so as not to wake him. As I plopped down, Hairy Joe shuffled in his slumber and muttered some unintelligible utterances. Trying to get comfortable, I thought about the letter in my pocket and pulled it out. It was difficult to decipher the faded words. Almost as quickly as I tried to read the mailing address, my fingers pinched the corners of the envelope and began to tear. My thoughts took me far from my immediate reality and if it weren't for the abrasive honking on the road, I would have been halfway through reading the letter. Upon awareness of my hands, I immediately stopped and growled to myself.

"What's that?" Joe was awake.

"Oh, it's nothing."

"Aren't you gonna open it?"

My lips remained shut.

"What if it's really important?" he added.

"Then the person I'm giving it to will be happy they got it, huh?"

"Did you write it? Are you thinking about not giving it?"

"The last letter I wrote was in eighth grade. A stupid assignment. You know, something like 'Write a letter to yourself from the future'; complete garbage."

"I used to love those creative pieces," Joe replied. I couldn't help but roll my eyes and turn the other direction. "What?" he continued, "I used to like them, is there anything wrong with that?"

"No, Joe, there isn't," I shook my head in disbelief. "Do you mind?"

"Mind what?"

"Leaving me alone."

"I'm sorry to try and engage you in some friendly conversation. It's not anything else is happening. We're just sitting here, waiting until the next stop," Joe said.

"Not me. I only want to be back home. There's no waiting. Here I am."

death letter blues

"People like you shouldn't even leave your homes. You only make things miserable for everyone else," Joe was starting to make a scene.

"Okay? I don't mind staying at home either. I don't even really know why I'm here. I don't even know why I'm actually talking to you," I couldn't help myself. The next three days next to this man are what I consider to be low-grade torture. They ought to change the bus company name to Guantanamo Express, Water board Travel, or even Sit Next to a Sweaty, Woolly Mammoth for Three Days and Watch Yourself Implode Motor Coaches. Joe's temple produced a bead of sweat that was quickly absorbed into the corner of his wriggling eyebrows. He turned his head away and anxiously continued to nibble his brittle cookies.

The road signs whizzed by in the night's dark, reflecting the headlights of the bus. The coach was filled with snoring travelers escaping the boredom with unfulfilled dreams. I wondered how many of them were too afraid to fly. No. They couldn't afford everything they needed to fly. They were just too poor. Their poverty made annoyed me. They used the bus lavatory and the nauseating odor would creep from the back to the front of the bus, permeating the air-conditioning system. It seemed to only bother me. I covered my nose. Passengers sitting in the back of the bus, completely immersed in the stench, leaned their sleeping domes on the walls of the bathroom. They took their shoes off for comfort and unknowingly caressed urine-logged pieces of toilet paper with their naked toes. They didn't know any better than to take their shoes off. I patted myself on the back for wearing combat boots in this testing ground for disease warfare: a petri dish of unconscious filth dragged from the bottom of some shoe on Fifth Street, traveling a mile a minute to the pulsing orifices of some kid whose parents never taught them how to wash their hands. GiGi never touched anything in my apartment.

death letter blues

"**K**noxville!" came from the overhead speakers, "Knoxville, Tennessee!" Shaggy Joe was startled by his own sleep apnea. When he opened his eyes, he looked through my window.

"Ahh! We're here. Finally," He sighed.

"You are here," I clarified. He just looked at me and began wrestling himself out of his abused seat. As he bent down to pick up some of his belongings from underneath his chair, rump in air, the unfortunate man released a fury of gas in my direction. I'm sure that some Yogi in northern India would suggest that this was a manifestation of a North American form of Karma; I would scoff, of course. There is a lot of doubt in my mind that some superior conscious being is taking moral tallies of every action that six billion people take and then ensures somehow the difference in good and evil doing remains balanced through a streak of bad luck. It smelled rotten.

The Knoxville bus station was equally wretched as the previous one. Dirty floors and savage passengers vying for place and position in a world that didn't care. Hordes of people pushed each other into some semblance of order to make sure their first-come first-served bus seat was secure. The advantage for me was a host of empty seats with adjoining television sets. This bus terminal hadn't changed since 1976, except for the added grime and grit that coated everything, including the civilians. I threw myself on one of the seats and began to pump quarters into the outdated, black and white, six-inch idiot box. After one dollar and fifty cents of repetitive feeding motions, it occurred to me that this box would not project moving images for me to stare into. Immediately, my clenched fist banged on the top and then on the sides. A profusion of vulgar utterances spilled from my mouth. People were staring; I could feel their glares with the tiny hairs on the back of my neck. Upon realizing my defeat, I helplessly melted into my seat, head in hand.

"Sir?" A hand gripped my shoulder from behind.

"Whatever it is you want is less important than why you're touching me." I faced the hand and then turned to notice the a tall, built, uniform-clad police officer eyeballing me. His head scanned me head to toe and back. He sported a thick Frank Zappa style mustache and wore aviator sunglasses indoors. I couldn't see his eyes, but I could feel the piercing judgment through the shades. Here I am, dark hair, dark eyes, and dark skin. He chewed some rancid smelling watermelon-mint combination bubble gum with what seemed like a lump of chewing tobacco. He spit on the floor and I knew I was in the South. I fucking hated the South.

"Is there a problem here?" He was making more of a statement than asking a question. I realized this and remained silent. "Your behavior is attracting a lot of attention."

"I'm out for a smoke," I stood and headed for the exit.

"Sir! Hold it right there."

"What do you want? I'm sorry! OK?" Clearly I was agitated.

"Sir! Please remain calm," the officer then coded something into his fuzzy sounding radio with his arm outstretched in a 'Halt!' position.

"Come talk to me outside. I'm going for a cigarette."

"Sir! Just stay here for now." His arm remained outstretched in my direction as he awaited a reply from voice on the other end of the radio. We stood there for a moment looking into each others' eyes. I knew it wasn't smart to look straight into this southern cop's eyes. It was really more like dealing with a wild bear than it was dealing with another human being. That line became increasing faded and gray with each passing day. You can't look a scary dog in the eyes because it feels threatened when you do that.

"Sir, that television set is private property. It doesn't belong to you. The nice folks 'round here think you're vandalizing it. You know what happens when you do that?"

"No."

death letter blues

"You get me," he tapped on his badge with the baton.

"OK."

"Why were you banging on it?"

"Because it ate my quarters. Talk to the machine."

"Did you talk to the folks at the information booth? Maybe they could get your money back?"

"I was just going to let it go."

"Then why'd you bang on it?"

"Because I was trying to get it to work. I want TV, not quarters. That's why I traded."

"How's that worked for you?" He continued without a response, "It looks like you need to control your anger."

"Control my anger?"

"Yes. Control it."

"I think 'angry' means 'out of control'. If I were keeping it under control, then I wouldn't be angry. I don't control my emotions; nobody does. It's impossible. And besides, I wasn't angry; I was frustrated, and there's no control for that. Tell the TV not to make me frustrated. Do that, and we don't have a problem."

elgazzar

"Sounds like Mr. Metro-City Man over here can't get his way with the television. Mr. City Man don't believe in self-control."

"Well, you guys are always banging on people trying to get them to work! Where's the self-control there? At least I don't have my foot on someone's neck and scream 'probable cause' to get them to respect me."

"Sir, don't use intimidating comments with me."

"Intimidating?"

"Sir, consider this your last warning."

"Warning? I didn't do anything wrong. What are you going to do? Take me in for being frustrated with the television set? I don't recall any laws against being frustrated."

"I've got a 6-4-7 in progress," the officer relayed into the radio. Some unintelligible fuzz returned from the radio. In one fell swoop I was being handcuffed and read my rights.

"What are you doing?! I've got a bus to catch!"

"You're being charged with disorderly conduct and obstruction of justice."

death letter blues

The police officer was leading me out of the bus terminal with the occasional "courtesy;" 'Lower your head, sir,' 'Lock your hands so the cuffs don't hurt as much, sir,' and 'This way, sir.' After we walked through the crowds he became less and less courteous. By the time we made it to the police car, he had a vice grip on my arm and then lunged me on to the hood of the cruiser. He forcefully patted me down and groped my balls. I squirmed. He yelled at me not to move or he would charge me with resisting arrest. He pulled my cigarettes, lighter, multiple wads of money, my passport, the god-forsaken letter, and my wallet out of my pockets and then dumped the rest of my change, receipts, tickets stub, and other random junk onto the sidewalk.

"Why do you have almost 2000 dollars on you?"

"I'm traveling cross country."

"Where are you headed to?"

"Montreal."

"Which one?"

"Un-fucking-real," I thought to myself. "Canada," I told him.

elgazzar

"Bernard Ruiz, huh? " He read off my passport. "What kind of name is that? It don't look like you're from these parts."

He then grabbed me and threw my carcass onto the backseat of the cruiser. He got in on the driver seat and fidgeted with computers, pens, papers, and gadgets that made beeping noises. He scribbled on some note pad and exited the vehicle. He came around, opened the door, and pulled me out and set me back on my feet. The officer carefully removed the handcuffs and nodded his head towards my belongings that were spread on the hood of the car and sidewalk. I shuffled to pick them up.

"How long until your bus leaves?"

"What time is it?"

The officer looked at his shiny watch. "Ten forty-five." I knew I missed the bus.

"Pretty soon."

"Good. We don't want people like you around here." He scribbled again on his notepad. "It's the end of my shift and I don't feel like taking you in. You wait in the bus station until your bus leaves and don't come back to Knoxville. Here's your warning." I nodded to him as he handed me some official documentation of his warning as if I were going to forget to get the hell out of Tennessee as fast as I could. "Now get on out of here."

"Redneck," the words escaped my mouth as I turned away.

"Watch your mouth, boy!"

"Watch your mother," I said under my breath as I launched a snotty hock onto the sidewalk. The cop was already in his car when I took my stand. It was probably a good thing that he didn't take notice of my impulses. I entered the building again.

The same hum of travelers, workers, bells and whistles resounded through the busy bus terminal halls. There was a clear path to the ticket window. The bus I was supposed to be on had already left and there was no real point in hurrying. The police officer had rattled me. Asshole. My mind attempted to stay focused on the ticket window but once I passed the television seats where I had previously positioned myself, I took notice of a young woman seated in my chair, watching my TV, using my quarters.

"Excuse me."

The young woman looked up at me and huffed, "What?"

elgazzar

"Did you put quarters in that machine?"

"No. It was already on. I sat down about twenty minutes ago and it had almost a full hour left on it."

"Yeah. They were mine."

"Sorry," she condescended. For a second I thought she was actually going to get up and cede the seat to me. When our eyes met for an awkward and unnecessary amount of time, I began to understand that she was waiting for me to leave. Either that or this was her completely unintelligible way of falling in love. My body made no moves; I just stood there, silently staring at the woman. She was attractive; no, she was beautiful. She had long brown hair that twisted and turned around the sharp features of her face. "What the fuck are you looking at?" She had edge too.

"You! I'm looking at you. You're out in public so I'm looking. You're sitting in my seat so I'm looking. You're using my quarters so I'm looking." Nothing else really needed to be said. I had nothing else to say.

"Listen, creep," she stood in face, "your name isn't written anywhere on this machine and there's no way you can prove that you put quarters in here. I just happened to walk by and see that some moron left a TV on so I sat down."

I continued to stand motionless, thinking of the degenerate policeman that had given me grief earlier. He could prove that I put quarters in there. For some odd reason, like maybe an army of officers hiding their uniforms under white sheets with pointy hoods and red trim ranting about the importance of diversity by preserving the purity and cleanliness of the race and avoiding, through murder, the abominations of mixed heritage; I just didn't feel like summoning the police. A giant burning cross somewhere in the middle of the Tennessee woods doesn't tickle my fancy. "I'm going to change my ticket," I said slowly, "and when I get back..."

"What? When you get back you can kiss my ass?" She signaled towards her wonderful round rump.

"When I get back, I'm going to sit down next to you and watch that damn TV. You can leave if you like, but I'm watching it." I was shrinking. In a swoop, I turned to the ticket booth. In reality, I didn't want her to leave, nothing depended on it, but I just wanted to watch TV with her. I could've sat down right there and then, but the idea of being in Tennessee was unappealing. It didn't sit right in my gut.

elgazzar

"Next!" The bus station employee summoned from behind his window.

"Hey. I need a new ticket. I missed the last bus."

"Where to?"

"Montréal," I cleared my throat and then continued, "Quebec."

"I know where Montreal is," he gave me a look.

I was speechless.

"Give me your old ticket." Silently I handed him the ticket. He snatched it from me and began a flurry of typing. Without a peep, I stood wondering what to do with my hands. In the pockets? Crossed in front of me? They ended up in my pockets. That was probably the most comfortable place for them. And of course, when I had almost completely forgotten, my hands made contact with that disagreeable piece of paper folded into an ancient envelope: that fucking letter always reminds me of itself in the most inopportune moments, like when I'm trying to focus on exchanging a bus ticket in the worst place in the world. The ticket guy was still typing.

"What are you typing?"

death letter blues

"I'm exchanging your ticket, what does it look like I'm doing?"

"Do you really want me to answer that?"

The bus station employee scratched his goatee and looked at me. "Yeah, answer the question."

"It looks like you're writing a novel or, um, maybe a Master's dissertation on the impatience of anxious travelers who need tickets exchanged in a hurry." I was definitely thinking about the girl. She could've colluded with this man to make sure that I wouldn't return to the TV set in time. That would've taken a bit of forethought. And since this man knew where the fuck Montreal was, he must've been a damn genius.

"Tomorrow morning."

"What do you mean 'tomorrow morning'?" I was confused.

"The bus leaves tomorrow morning." He must've pulled a fast one on me.

"No."

"Tomorrow morning. That's it. Here's your new ticket and here's the old one." He stamped a huge, red

'VOID' on the old ticket, stapled it to the new one and slid them both underneath the glass.

When I returned to the TV sets, the girl was gone. My seat was open though and it looked like the TV was still running. I made myself comfortable, crossed my legs, and tried to mentally shut myself down. The TV shut off. What? I just sat down! What a hoax. Again, I was left with myself. Watching people and waiting for buses gets old and boring. Is it possible for a man to exhaust all his thoughts? It was probably good that the girl with the brown hair had left. If we weren't fighting, I would've been annoyed with her. Anything she had to say would've bored me. Besides the superficial courtesies that people pay each other in order to get what they want, and what they want in themselves, there isn't much else to talk about. That's what brought me to her: she wasn't much for niceties. It's the courtesies that shudder through my being, the 'Hi' and 'Bye' and 'Thank you' and 'Oh my God!' and 'Please' and 'How are you?'

death letter blues

The hard plastic seat at the Knoxville Bus Station absorbed me.   For about an hour, a heap of arms and legs wriggled in this uncomfortable space.   Eventually, they settled. Half at rest, half dead. Only the occasional twitch in my hand or passing janitor would remind me that I was here. I wish I could say I was thinking about something.

elgazzar

death letter blues

Cautious not to run into the swift sword of the law again, I made my way to the front door and lit up. Two guys were standing outside. One was big, the other was small.

"Gotta light?" The large one turned to face me. My arm was outstretched and I snapped the lighter. "Hey, what's your name, man?"

"B."

"I think I seen you around. I'm Reggie and this here's Li'l Green." Li'l Green wore baggy camouflage fatigues and a lime green beanie.

"Why do they call 'im 'green'?"

"It's a long story man. He can tell you if he wants to, but he don't say much." He turned and patted Green on the arm, "Tell 'im why dey call you green." Green looked at me with a don't-give-me-that-shit-you-know-damn-well expression. I looked back at Reggie and took a drag off my smoke.

"What time is it?"

"*Late*. Why? You waitin' on a bus?"

"Yeah."

"Where to?"

"Montréal." I was getting bored with this question.

"I've been up to Montréal once or twice. I went when I turned eighteen. You know, drinkin' and playin' cards. Nice people up there, 'cept for the uppity types. They messed with me. Now, you ain't Black like me, but you're dark. They gon' fuck with you."

"They mess with me right here."

death letter blues

"True, but the way they mess with you is different. In Tennessee, people let you know that they don't like you, but they know that it ain't cool to be racist 'n' shit. And then in Detroit, like where I'm from, there's a lot of 'hood, so nobody has to mix. But up in Montréal, where it's the last stop on the Underground Railroad, you get off that train and they make a fashion out of not liking you. You know, Toronto ain't like that. People is cool in Toronto. But that European thing they got goin' on up there, that shit is racist as fuck." Reggie had a lot to say on that.

"They don't lynch people up there though."

"Yeah. That's 'cause they take your ass right off the train and won't let you in the country."

"Hmmm," I thought for a moment, "But you got to go."

"Yeah!" Reggie bust out laughing', tapped Li'l Green on the arm and looked back, "I got laid too."

"How'd you do in the casino?"

"I lost man," Reggie got serious, "Ain't nobody ever win at the casino." He paused. "Why? You like to play?"

"Sometimes, not really."

"Well, shit, we can get a game on right now!" Reggie glanced at a nodding Green. "What do you think?"

"Nah, man. I got a bus to catch."

"Man, C'mon! What do you play? Blackjack? Dice? Stud? What?"

"It's cool, man. I don't think I'm playin'. What time is it anyway?"

"It's *early* man. We can have some fun before you get your ride. What else are you gonna do? Stay around that nasty bus station forever?!"

"You guys go ahead. I'm gonna sit this one out."

"No use playin' just the two of us." Reggie and the outspoken Green just stood there.

"Where you going to anyway?"

"Montréal."

"Yeah, that's right." Reggie, Li'l Green, and I fell into an awkward silence.

death letter blues

"Let me see that lighter." Li'l Green broke the hush. I lit his cigarette and we resumed our frozen stances. I thought for sure that whenever Li'l Green actually spoke, it would be a life altering, spiritual, awakening for me. No such thing.

"I'm headed back inside. Bye." The two men watched me turn towards the building.

elgazzar

death letter blues

There was no way to find out how many more bus stations I would have to visit before arriving at my destination. Headed North; through Michigan or Upstate New York? Either way I would find myself in quasi-Midwestern-almost-East Coast-soon-to-be-but-not-actual cities like Cincinnati or Pittsburgh. Pretty cities, aesthetically, but once you get past the deceptive façades, there's nothing but denial; denial of brutal cops, how uncool the people actually are, and how little there is to do.

elgazzar

The candy machine baited me and I dropped some quarters in. Without doubt, the spiral rows, lined with chocolate bars, sticks of gum, and dusty bags of chips, would jam on the wrappers of F-6. Everyone I know has lost money in those damn machines. Some folks pump in more quarters to fool themselves into a two-for-one deal. The real dedicated consumers trudge through numerous conversations until they nag the one person who possesses the key to the machine; they get their seventy-five cents, but are never reimbursed for their time. Of course, I was right: my cheetos dangled upside-down like a sport climber who just missed a hold. Soon the chips would resume their course towards what they were always intended to do: be eaten. Just not right now. Looking around the vacant terminal with only the rhythmic hum of all the gadgetry as company, I reached in my pockets and dumped some more change in the slot machine. I pulled the lever and watched two bags drop to the bottom of the window. My mouth expanded and I hurled the snacks in. It was a vulgar affair.

Through the front door, the street slowly became overrun with morning light and commuters. People gradually ushered themselves into the bus station. The humans oozing into the building signaled my approaching departure; the driver would show up, the bus would refuel, and more passengers would be taken on. There's no way I'm getting on another bus. This'll be the last. Once I get to my next destination, I'll try and get on a train.

"Lexington, Cincinnati, Indianapolis, Chicago!" A uniformed man hollered into the half-empty halls. I proceeded to the gate and joined in the bottlenecking. There was no real queue, just another mass of bodies funneling through the doorway, showing tickets in hand and pulling their luggage behind them. It reminded of some third-world food drive: a bunch of malnourished stick figures massacring each other for first dibs on the rice truck. Poor bastards. My seat on the bus was waiting for me. A sigh of relief overtook me as I plopped down in the chair. It was the first soft, padded, cushioned entity I had come across in quite sometime except for Fuzzy Joe. Everything else was calloused and edgy.

When the bus began to pull out, it was pleasing to know that nobody was sitting next to me. Hills turned to Mountains and then back to hills. This was Kentucky: pedigree horses, bluegrass, and rednecks. Other than rednecks, I didn't see much else besides what they had printed on the giant billboards that lined the highways. Abortion Stops a Beating Heart. Jesus Loves You. Fireworks. Support Our Troops. John Deere. The National

elgazzar

Rifle Association: Don't shoot until you see the rags on their heads. It was wrong to be here. Despite poverty, abandonment, and famine, rural Americans are too wrapped up in the ideas of democracy, liberty, and freedom to cooperatively do anything about it. The *real* Americans. The Americans that just don't get it. Getting across the Ohio River seemed more important now than ever. But how much does a river prevent ideological diffusion from occurring?

We stopped for about thirty minutes in Lexington. I didn't bother getting off the bus. There was obviously nothing to see. I knew that before I got here. But when I saw a small group of Black guys smoking cigarettes, I figured I could do the same.

The cigarette burned bright, the fumes entered me and then left me. Calmness. Two more drags. One more drag. Drop the smoke. Step on it. Get back on the bus. Sit down. I knew this routine. Soon, the bus leaves.

death letter blues

It took three hours to travel ninety miles from Lexington to Cincinnati. Fucking ridiculous. The skyline from above the hills approaching the city was inspiring, although only for about as long as we held the view, which was momentary. We descended into the Ohio River valley and crossed the river. Five minutes after, officially entering "The North", since Kentucky didn't know what to do with itself during the Civil War, we stopped at the bus station. But where was the train station? Stepping out the building, there was a huge parking lot surrounding the terminal and

elgazzar

covering about three full city blocks. The parking lot was contained with a highway to the east, semi-skyscrapers to the south, and a line of old Italianate row houses to the west and north.

"Hey, lady, where's the train station around here?" I asked a little old lady that clutched her purse as I lit up.

"Please?"

"What? Please?" She walked away. What just happened? I looked around a bit more. For a city that boasts a number of Fortune 500 companies, two fully professional sports teams with stadiums, and hosts at least three or four universities, not a soul was walking the streets near the bus station. An older white man inside a glass box was collecting fees from vehicles exiting the car park. He didn't see me approach and when I rasped on the two-inch thick, bulletproof glass, he abruptly turned to face me.

"What do you want?" People here were very friendly.

"Is there a train station around here?"

"Yes," He looked me in the eye through his thick glasses. Anticipating further explanation, I just stood there. He said nothing.

"You wouldn't mind sharing that information with me, would you?"

"It's straight across town. Take a cab or take a bus or something," he waved me away in some general direction.

"Can I walk there?"

"You can walk anywhere. But I wouldn't," A very concerned look exaggerated his already enlarged eyeballs through the magnifying power of his VISION 2000 glasses. A slight chuckle escaped me.

"Is it far?"

"It's dangerous. That right there," he pointed towards the row houses, "it's all ghetto." He shook his finger at me again, "take a cab or something."

"You make it seem like Compton or Harlem."

"Please?"

"What? *Please*?"

"I'm working here. Go on, get outta here," he handed some change back to the passing driver and shut the sliding window in my face. My body stood there, erect but confused. The old man just stared straight ahead and tapped a silent beat on the cash register. I knocked on the glass. Not even a blink from the old man. What a poker face! I knocked again. Nothing. I walked to the front of the box, directly in his line of vision, and repeatedly slammed my open palms on the glass. Nothing. I cursed him and gestured indignantly before walking away at full pace. He made me angry. He gritted my teeth. My arms waved in the air maniacally and I bellowed a roar of irritability. My legs headed me in the direction of the row houses. I didn't know where I was going, just walking, moving. A cloud of annoyance shielded me. It felt like I was floating on that haze, through the buildings, through the streets. People sat on their stoops, knowing I wasn't from the neighborhood, eyeballing me, head to toe and back. Nobody did anything. Just people hanging out on their stoops.

Several people along the way gave me directions and slowly made way towards the train station. A long, wide concourse spilled out onto the steps of a huge Beaux-Arts half-dome with a fountain and a cul-de-sac passenger drop off area. I walked inside. An enormous mosaic of what seemed like a Leninist era mural of steelworkers helping each other dominated the interior of the dome. There were signs pointing to the theater, museum, and gift shop. Where was I? The information booth directed me downstairs.

"I gotta get to Montréal."

"Canada?" Without looking up from the computer screen, the worker requested more information.

"Yes."

"OK," she punched in a few more keys, "It leaves tomorrow at 6:00 pm."

"You'll get off in Cleveland and catch the connection to Schenectady, New York. Get off in Schenectady and catch the Northern directly to Montréal."

"What time is it now?" My head bobbed and turned looking for a clock.

"It's almost four." She paused, "It'll be 349 dollars."

"Damn!"

"Please?" The look on her face was intense. The edges of her eyes burned with ire.

"I'm just sayin', you know, it's expensive. It's not much quicker than a bus."

elgazzar

"The seat is a *helluvalot* more comfortable and you can move around."

"Can I smoke?"

"You can't smoke anywhere in the U.S." She stopped for a moment and tapped on her jacket pocket, "it's a shame too. I gotta go outside to smoke, and if I don't clock out, my pay gets docked."

"How much is it again?" A wad of folded money appeared from one of my many pockets.

"380 dollars."

"A minute ago you said something else. And that's when you told me about the auto-massaging recliner and the on board gymnasium."

"Looks like Uncle Sam wants a cut." She had a shrill chuckle. I shelled over the money, got the ticket and walked out of the building.

The sun was beginning to set outside. There wasn't much traffic around the train station. I guess not many people were interested in the antiquated railroad system. I couldn't say why the trains haven't been refurbished since the Chinese, but I know that the automotive industry, airline companies, and federal government are in constant

death letter blues

collusion. Bailouts, subsidies, and corporate welfare. I continued down the wide concourse past the fountain and into the industrial sector of the city. I headed towards the tall buildings a couple miles off.

When I got downtown, there wasn't much to take note of: empty one-way streets criss-crossing large vacant buildings with lights on. I heard some faint music playing in a nearby club. After scanning the surrounding blocks, a bouncer appeared, sitting on a stool, smoking a cigarette. As I approached the door, the bouncer, sporting a sharp fedora, opened his palm towards me as if begging for money or food or something. I shook his hand instead.

"I.D., man! I ain't tryin' to say 'wassup?'" He pulled his hand away from me.

"Oh." I gave him my passport.

"What's this?"

"It's a passport." I replied.

"A passport?"

"Yeah, a passport. You wanted I.D., right?"

"Man! I can't accept this. I need some official state identification or something."

elgazzar

"This is a Federal, United States I.D., This is the I.D.; I can travel to different countries with this. Custom officers and Immigration officials scan these in to see if you're legit. INS hounds people for these."

"Well, this is Cincinnati, and you tryin' to get into a club here. This ain't a different country. So if you ain't got no state I.D., go away, you ain't gettin' in."

"Damn, man. Let me talk to someone."

"You can talk to me."

"Get me the manager."

"She ain't here."

"You want to me get the police? Just to prove that this is legit?"

"We don't need no *mo'fuckin' po*-lice 'round here!"

"Then let me in!"

"Five bucks cover." He opened his palm again and I dropped some money into it. "Go on."

As the low lights and the smoke of the club engulfed me, the chatter immediately ceased. It smelled the same way as my cheesy, first Steve Miller concert: weed. Only the music continued to play. My body froze in motion. Everyone in the club was staring me.

death letter blues

"Excuse me," a man bumped into me.

"It's cool," I said. The commotion, conversations, and merriment resumed. People made way for me as I approached an empty table and chair combination with a lit candle sitting atop it.

"What can I getcha?" The waitress asked. And she was beginning to work me over.

"How 'bout a bourbon. On the rocks," I paused, "Nah, make it neat," I paused again. "You know what," I continued, "Make it a double."

"You sure?"

"Yeah, I think so."

"You want anything else?" She looked me up and down and then stared right into my eyes.

"Ashtray, maybe?"

"Anything else?"

"I'm alright for now, I think," I took my eyes away until she turned around and started back to the bar area. I couldn't help but watch her every step, shake, and giggle. She turned a corner and the band caught my attention. Two old folks were playin' the blues. It's really the only way to hear old blues. One was an old man, dressed in an old, dusty, gray suit, missing teeth and fingers, but pouring his heart out on an electric piano plugged into the PA system. The other was an old woman, draped in an old 1930's flapper dress, a hat with a mesh veil and fake flower tucked in her curls. She was playing a two-piece drum set: tapping on a snare and a high-hat. They were jamming on some old Son House tune about a boy that realized he loved a girl only when they began to bury her. But I couldn't really understand a word of it. The rest of the club was packed with thirty or forty-somethings that just wanted to get drunk and laugh. They were fucking loud. It was hard to listen to the music. But then again, these establishments weren't built around the music. The music is just a ploy to get people in the club while the genius of the music just gets lost in the humdrum of the audience. There's so much passing me by.

The liquor burned my throat but it felt nice. Each sip sent a feverish jolt through my body and I would sigh after each one. Slowly my body began to sink into lifelessness and observation. My being became camouflage, consisting of only a set of passive eyes, watching the motion patterns and hearing indiscernible sounds.

death letter blues

"You doin' alright?" The waitress comes by every now and then to check on me. Sometimes I just nod and say 'yes' or ask her to bring me another drink. The small encounters with the server occasionally reintegrate me into my surroundings; she reminds me that I am still subject to the external world. For only momentary lapses of dreaminess, my environment makes me aware. The eighty-year olds on the small stage began to wane. The music took a deeper, more down-tempo turn.

"Honey?" the waitress poked, "we're shutting down in a bit. Last call."

The crowd in the room was beginning to thin. The dawdlers desperately leaned over the bar counter, struggling to keep their heads up, imploring the bartender to pass one more drink. He obliged them. My hand gestured 'another'. She brought my whiskey, one for herself, and sat down.

"We're closed," she said. "You gotta leave soon."

"Just this drink," I lifted the tumbler.

"Cheers," she nodded at me and we clinked our glasses. As far and I was concerned, there really wasn't much to discuss so I said nothing. She seemed a bit uneasy. "What's your name?" she asked.

elgazzar

"B."

"Where you from, B?"

"Around."

"Nah. You're not from 'round here? I been here all my life and I woulda seen you at least once. Whatchu doin' in this town?"

"Waiting for a train."

"When does it leave?"

"Tomorrow night."

"So you got some time. I'm Ciara." We shook hands.

"Hey, C!" A loud bellow originated from the large bartender, "Are we shuttin' down or what?" suggesting that she help count the register and wipe down the bar.

"Finish your drink," she pointed at my glassful. By the time I turned back to face her, she was already at the register with her accountant hat on: literally, a dark, wire-mesh baseball hat that read Don't Bug the Accountant with a small graphic of a larger ladybug either feeding or trampling three smaller ladybugs. She was focused and driven, perhaps a bit compartmentalized, but she knew what she needed to do. Ciara took things seriously: she organized her life. She probably had dreams too. Who wants to push alcohol and clean up after others the rest of their lives? She's making good tips and saving some money. Who knows what for? New dress? New car? New hairdo? New kids? Old rent?

My glass was empty. I walked towards to Ciara to settle the debt on the booze. "How much do I owe you?"

"Five drinks at five bucks a piece. So... twenty-five." She stopped counting all the assorted stacks of denominations. I reached in my pocket and pulled out my wad of bills. Her eyes traced my movements. My fingers riffled through some of the bills. Without looking I handed her one of them. "You want change?" she asked.

"Hmm? Oh? No." What was wrong with me? To avoid any other embarrassment in my present state, my body rotated, bound for the exit.

"Hey! Wait! Are you sure you don't want change? You gave me a fifty." She yelled after me. Gradually, it seemed, I came to a halt and again, my body rotated. She was walking towards me with some cash in her hand.

"This is a big tip."

"No. It's OK," I said.

elgazzar

"Where you goin' right now?"

"Outside."

"I can't let you go out on your own in that state. Besides, you ain't from here. Where you gonna stay? You got a room somewhere or somethin'?"

Somehow, I managed to shrug my shoulders.

"I got a room you can rent for the night. It'll cost ya fifty bucks plus the cab ride there. What do you say?"

My palms opened onto my head. I rubbed and contorted the skin on my face.

"You're coming with me," she said underneath her breath and kindly, but firmly, grabbed my underarm and led me towards the door. She continued, "I'll get the cab ride with the tip you just gave me, but you better pay up in the morning."

death letter blues

The screeching tires of the halting cab awoke me from a slumber. There was a dream of being back in my apartment, smoking cigarettes and ashing in the pizza box. I looked up to see Ciara riding next to me and giving directions to the driver. "No, No. It's the next block. Keep going," she would say as she tapped her long fingernail on the inside of the taxi's window.

"Right here."

"Right there?"

elgazzar

"Yeah, right here. Here." She pulled me out of the car. My empty vessel of a corpse just followed along with the motions that she was guiding me through. We entered a brick building through a series of security doors forming an airlock or some sort of small, contained foyer. She fidgeted with the locks and led me into a narrow stairwell going up. As she led, I noticed her round rump was more noticeable now from a couple steps below than when we were at the club. She kept looking over her shoulder to me, smiling, winking; she was a flirt. After what seemed like an infinite, but enjoyable, amount of steps, she finally stopped in front of a door marked 4-B. We walked in. The apartment had an open space with three adjacent doors: kitchen, bathroom, and bedroom. Ciara led me to the bedroom and threw me on the bed. When she flipped the lights on, I noticed her tan skin and full features.

"Take your damn shoes off. I just washed my sheets," she commanded me with all the authority of a madame of a whorehouse. The boots haven't come off my feet for several days. It was a good thing I was drunk and unable to respond physically to the smell of my musty feet nor socially to the embarrassment of knowing that I smelled horrible.

death letter blues

"You wanna take a shower or something?" Ciara asked. It seemed like such a chore. "Go on," she continued. I watched my body stumble to the shower. I just stood in the water for a few minutes. When I got done, the dust and sweat of the last several days dripping off of every extremity, no towel was to be found. From what appeared to be a distant observation of myself, there was panic. Weary not to call for Ciara and explain the embarrassing predicament I found myself in as if pleading for toilet paper after eating dairy products, my open hands slowly swept my body, leaving only a light film of moisture that had set into my skin. The result was simple: use my soiled undershirt to pat down the wettest spots then flag it over the shower curtain bar to dry. Unclear as to why I cared so much about drying myself, I walked out of the hospital-like bathroom completely nude, leaving a steaming pile of my clothes on the shower rug on the middle of the floor. Most of the lights in the apartment were turned off which made the trek from the bathroom to the bedroom nearly impossible. I must've bumped my forehead three times on low overhead, stubbed my big toe at least twelve times on misplaced furniture, and frantically held my arms out like a madman for the duration of the journey. Eventually I made it to the bedroom and when I stubbed my toe for the very last time, I found the bed and fell upon it with the greatest respect to gravity. My head landed on the pillow. Immediately, I couldn't discriminate between fantastic wakefulness and rousing, vivid dreams. Ciara spoke to me, trying to maneuver intellectually and sexually with me. I didn't notice any response of my own. Surely, I was asleep.

"Hey!" Ciara shrieked and firmly nudged me; "You aren't really falling asleep on me?"

Some sort of groan was issued from my gut.

"Get up!" She yelled again.

Nothing.

"What's wrong with you? You're in my house! Now wake up!" Despite her insistence, I did not reply, I could not reply. My eyes were shut, but I could sense her pacing the room. The rhythm of her footsteps and the high-pitch whistle of the cool draft brought me to the purgatory uniting fantasy and reality.

death letter blues

A ray of light smashed through the window and settled on my face; similar to the way it did back in my own apartment. My head turned on the pillow and I knew I was awake. I faked my sleep for a while but caved in to the idea of getting up when it dawned on me where I was: Ciara's place. Sitting up, I scanned the room but she wasn't there.   She wasn't in the living room either... or the kitchen... or the bathroom. There was a pile of drab clothes in the bathroom; right... my own... which meant I was naked.

elgazzar

Dressing myself was a whirlwind of an undertaking. The pockets of my jacket, one in particular, felt unusually light. Some money was missing. Maybe last night I was loose with my allowance; the taste of alcohol did still saturate my breath. Could Ciara have stolen from me? Would she have robbed me? Of course... it's human nature. After counting through all my cachés, there was about a thousand and some change left. I definitely spent a lot last night and I definitely got robbed. There was no letter. I lost the letter! A vision of GiGi's henchmen suddenly haunted me. Frantically, I raced around her apartment, checking in drawers full of junk: scotch tape, playing cards, cheap jewelry (that found it's way to my pockets... human nature), and drink coasters with Impressionist prints. The bedroom dresser drawers were full of shorts and t-shirts. The bedside tables hid an exhaustive collection of arousing lingerie and erotic toys. The letter was tucked into the side of the drawer. After stuffing the envelope into one my pockets, I sighed. Motionless and dumbfounded, I wondered whether to bag the sexy stockpile or just stare at it. Really, this shit costs a lot of money, although I don't think many pawnshops really want to purchase that kind of used product. When I heard the front door slam shut, I snapped into a frenzied race to shut the drawers and appear innocent.

"You still here?" It was Ciara. "What are you doing? You shoulda been gone by now!"

"You took money from me," I said.

"What?! No, you gave me money. The ride, rent, the shower, the bed, and all that."

"All that?"

"Yeah. Well... it wasn't all that since you didn't even fuck me 'cause you were drunk."

I sighed relief. Not that I wouldn't jump at the opportunity to knock boots with the lady, but I would've much rather been awake and present for it, participating freely and mentally documenting special moments as they happened so that I could recall them and masturbate when there was nobody around.

"So what were you doing in my drawers?" She marched through the flat, examining each drawer, jar, and box.

"So where's my money?"

"You still accusing me of stealing your money?!" Ciara replied.

"Well, I got a lot less here than I had before."

"Get the fuck outta my house!" She rushed me, grabbed me by the wrist, and tugged at me, all while pushing me out of the front door. Virtually free of provocation, her shrill tone rose with her temper. She hurled a storm of insults at me, almost in a language I didn't understand. The words Motherfucker, limp-dicked, faggot, cum-dumpster, and cheap were arranged in such a way as to indicate to the recipient, in this case... me, that she had taken offense to the fact that I was uninterested, despite my current arousal, in her greatest attempt at seduction; and then continued to scream these false assertions through the hallways of her building all the way down to the street exit. Needless to say, I raced down the steps to distance myself from her. When I got to the front door, a large man, whom somehow I must've overlooked on my way in, blocked the escape. He held one hand out in a 'Halt!' position towards me as I approached.

"Wait right here," he said in a calm that exuded confidence and concern. Ciara's high-heel pattering was getting louder and her piercing voice was nearer. "Are you alright, Ciara?" The doorman asked.

death letter blues

"This here {blah, blah, blah, blah, blah} is accusing me of stealing his money even though I let him come up in my bed, shower..." There was clearly no hope for an end to Ciara's ranting, "... and then he didn't fuck me like a real man..."

The doorman silently chuckled to himself at my expense and interrupted the woman, "So, you're alright?"

"Of course I'm fucking alright! This {blah, blah, blah, blah, blah} can't do shit to me! I own him..."

My eyes conveyed to the big man no sense of malice despite an urgency to escape this humiliating and ceaseless tirade. I felt like I wanted to piss. He moved out of my way, after ensuring that the woman was safe, and I jetted into the street cautious to make sure I shut the door behind me, and inhaled four or five cigarettes.

I hailed the first cab I could find, which took twenty-five minutes, and then the driver didn't even stop. The neighborhood seemed rough, more shady characters mean-mugging me. My adrenaline was pumping after the Ciara affair, which potentially, could've ended my life on two fronts: the big man at the door and almost losing my beloved letter. Nobody messed with me, they could tell I wasn't in the mood and I full of untapped trouble. Morality

103

elgazzar

dictates a passive, non-violent approach to screeching women, but angry and aggressive men rightfully deserve vigilant torture and assault.

Since cabdrivers indignantly refuse to slow down, let alone stop, in low-income or minority communities, there were no other options than to just walk. Only complete idiots wouldn't be able to read my emotional tells; only idiots would get in my face right now. It was precisely my short-fused appearance that held people at bay. That worked for me. Most of the businesses in this area were shut down and boarded up. If all the businesses operated without viable markets, with all government subsidies bailing out already wealthy Wall Street speculators who gamble and lose with other peoples' money, of course economy would dwindle and die. Besides, if people are worrying about buying bread and diapers, who the hell is putting money aside for the finer luxuries of life: small electronics, escargot, and barista concocted coffees. Mmmm, coffee. That sounded good.

death letter blues

Call it 'sadism', call it what you will, rich people deserve hell. You might spot one standing at the bus stop, stiff and erect with the worst kind of smugness and insecurity. Once the grey poupon collects its inheritance, it builds walls around the fear of sharing with the havenots: smelly white-trash-rag-head-wet-back-nigger-spick-queer-refugees from some long-lost, exotic, military regime by the beach. Most wealthy people, desperate to protect all they earn, are born into granddaddy's hard earned riches, are educated in the finest universities without scholarship or merit, and then perpetuate their prosperity by paying someone else to push overpriced products onto an uninterested, but addicted, market. So what do they care about positive social change? Fat cats haven't tapped the bottomless money-pit of hope, change, and peace. Well... not yet anyway... imagine that... forced at gunpoint to buy hope, change and peace at $19.99 each. Impossible. I suppose it's all intended for and justified by community service. Then again, I've never volunteered; there isn't much one person can do. The suit standing next to me waiting for the crosstown bus has a white-knuckle vice-grip on his briefcase.

What I really wanted to do was scare the businessman with a quick 'Boo!' But then what? Would I threaten the man with a clenched fist and demand he show me the contents of the briefcase? While I was interested in why he was gripping it so tight, had he given it to me, I wouldn't know what to do with it. The black leather satchel could've been filled with cash, jewels, important documents, or whatever. Nothing in that bag would get me to Montréal quicker. Even if the secrets of teleportation were documented in the folds of his briefcase, we would still have to wait on the idea's physical construction, training, methodology. That takes time. Of course, a flight

death letter blues

is out of the question. Had we preferred airports and security and, needless to say, sitting in a cabin magically suspended at thirty-thousand feet, the envelope would be delivered and I could get back to brooding aimlessly in the comfort of home (and no matter how much people say they understand aerodynamic jargon: thrust, lift, drag, Reynolds number, Mach; they just can't explain it to normal people in any sensible way).

Anyway, I shelled out a few bucks at a coffee shop with rigid wire chairs that dig into the middle of the back. The discomfort forced me to leave the trendy café and enter the chili parlor across the street and down the way. The staff suggested a three-way or a coney for first timers as they tied a bib around my neck and sat me down. Within exactly one-minute of my seating, the entire restaurant staff bustled to dish up my entire order plus a glass of water that I didn't ask for. The "chili" consisted of spaghetti; a sweet, dark, runny, sauce with chunks in it; and a mound of finely shredded cheddar cheese that you could barely see over. It all ended up in my gut. I removed the bib, payed the bill, asked for directions, and walked to the train station. Not much seemed to happen today, not that there was any need for more excitement; it was mostly walking from place to place, but time flew. It was already getting dark.

elgazzar

The thought of sitting on a train as opposed to a bus excited me: wider seats, long walks through the cars. Engine car... Passenger car... Dining car... Smoking car... Gymnasium car... Swimming pool car... Caboose... Foreign kids could kick-off full-size soccer matches in the spaces between the seats. There's no need to redesign trains for more space, just add another car. Finally, the huge arch-slash-dome of a train depot was just ahead. I didn't bother stopping at the information desk since I had already found the stairwell that led to the boarding platforms. There were no passengers waiting there. Even if there are only a few travelers, they tend to show up early to ensure passage. But, again, nobody was waiting.

There was a chain-link fence separating the train platforms from what appeared to be a parking lot and a bus stop. There were some folks standing around there. There would be no harm in asking them if they were going north.

"Is anyone going though Cleveland?" I hollered through the fence.

"Yup," someone yelled back.

"The six P.M.?"

"Yup."

death letter blues

When I got to the information desk to ask about the train, the woman told me there was no train.

"What do you mean 'there is no train'?"

"There's no train between here and Cleveland."

"But yesterday, I bought an Amtrak ticket to Montréal through Cleveland and... Schu-nec-..."

"Schenectady?"

"Yeah. She told me that it leaves tonight at six P.M."

"Yeah, the bus service connection to Cleveland leaves from the bus stop at six P.M."

"But it's a train ticket?"

"There are no trains between here and Cleveland."

"Then why did she sell me a train ticket?"

"Because it's an Amtrak bus service connection."

This conversation was beginning to go round and round in circles. Silently, I stood in front of the information booth. There was no point in fighting back to recover some dignity from the humiliating ruse that the ticketeers had pulled.

"Well, is there a train in Cleveland?" I asked

"Yup, it's direct to Schenectady."

"How long is the ride to Cleveland?"

"Oh... It's about four or five hours."

"Which one?"

"It depends."

"On what?"

"...On how many stops it has to make."

"Couldn't you check on the computer or something?"

"Sir, if you keep asking me questions, you're going to miss the bus. I think it's leaving now."

death letter blues

About five and a half hours later, after dropping off and picking up at numerous Amish and Quaker communities, the bus pulled into the Cleveland Bus station. There was a cool chill coming in from the lake. The platforms stretched parallel to the Erie shore. I popped my collar to protect my neck and without thinking, I was already blowing smoke. The ticket said I had one hour until the next train departed. There was no reason to leave the station.

elgazzar

Down the way a man was playing an old Stratocaster guitar. He traveled with a small, portable, Pignose amplifier. He was slim; tight black jeans, tight white tee, black button-up with the sleeves rolled up, and topped with a black hat. Nice hat; very nice hat. I happen to possess a peculiar fancy for hats. All different kinds of hats: top hats, fedoras, 10-gallons, beanies, skullcaps, tropics, bowlers, tukes, yarmulkes, and bonnets. This particular fellow was wearing a Texas-made, handwoven, Gammage Hi-Roller and this particular hat was made of black hare-fur felt. Soft. Durable. Nice hat. If I were so bold as to make such a public statement of true taste, I would definitely have to fold over money for the one hundred percent beaver fur. His hat was nice, but the beaver fur lasts even longer and keeps the head even warmer. My Hi-Roller would have sixteen conchos across the saddle; his had only eight. My brim would go out flatter with a more accented finger roll on the edge. This lucky bastard actually has the stones to wear that thing. Nice fucking hat. I wanted to tell him what I thought of his hat, but I didn't want to know the story of how he got it. It wasn't a gift from your ex's mother, so you don't have to wear it all the time. You just want people to know that's why it's part of your identity. You and the hat are inseparable. But it's not like you had a deep, harmony-epiphany with a kindred spirit at a Rainbow gathering and this is a memento that you stole. Just tell the fucking truth: you went to the store and bought that thing because you thought it was cool. This guy with his hat was a spectacle. He was always performing; he had no down time, no "time to take off the hat" and just be. Guitar players, especially lead musicians, make great actors and impersonators with over-the-top facial expressions. The intoxicated audience thinks to itself, {*cheering*,} "Man, he looks like he's jammin'!" They wave their hands in the air and dance to a rhythm of their own; it's mostly white people who drink lots of beer, wear L.L Bean gear (if that hasn't been replaced by J. Crew yet), and sport white "bar" hats with their favorite college mascots embroidered across the front. The technique and "care" with which they break their hats in necessitates truly skilled labor. The only thing I know about the elaborate process is the first step: Listen to Jack Johnson or Dave Matthews.

"You play?" He asked me as he gestured to the instrument.

"Me? Nah."

"I take it you're waiting for the train too," he said.

"Yeah. We got a little bit of time."

"Where you headed?" he asked.

"Montréal."

"Nice," he replied.

And an awkward silence took us. He looked around and strummed the fiddle a bit.

"Well, I'm going to New York City."

"Uh-Huh," was all I muttered with a nod as I pulled off my smoke.

"I'm gonna cut a record," he said with all his youthful exuberance. It was a bit shocking to hear somebody actually say that... Cut a record. His words felt like a time warp to the late 1920's on a dusty road somewhere in Mississippi. This young guy going to New York City must've just sold his soul to the devil and excited to share with the world what eternal hellfire can bring. I bet it's an impressive affair; a unique and innovative addition to the guitar virtuoso world. Something I've never heard. Maybe it's the devil that gave him the hat. You know, "something to remember me buy. 'Cause one of these days I'll be back to collect my dues."

"Good luck with that," I said.

"Oh, well, luck ain't got nothin' to do with it," he argued.

"Alright... well... then have fun with it."

"That's exactly what I intend to do," he turned with both hands held out towards the east along the railroad tracks, "Gonna have some fun!" He picked up his guitar, plugged it in, and began to play gentle melodies as passengers slowly showed up on the platform. He signaled me to hand him a cigarette. I obliged. After all, this guy just sold his soul. You can have the whole pack.

"Name's Johnny," he gave me a standard handshake but then lowered his head in a very polite, almost east Asian way. "Nice to meet you," he said. I nodded back to him. "You got a name?"

"B."

"B? Huh? I kinda like that."

"Thanks."

"I might have to use that: 'Johnny B.'" He was definitely a performer; a new character every day.

"Man, that's my name. Besides, your mom must've given you a name."

115

"What do you know about me?" He was annoyed; I think it was the 'mom' reference. He went on; "My life's gone on this far without the likes of you. I've been all around and you don't even know."

"Then tell me a story!" I said, raising the bet.

"I sold my soul," he said without any hesitation.

"What?" shocked in disbelief.

"I sold my soul."

"I heard you... b... but," I stuttered, "...nevermind."

"Say it," he demanded, "I told you something."

"What did you buy with it?"

"Something special."

"Hmm, what did it cost you?"

"Eternity."

"Eternity? What if life sucks?"

"It used to, but it doesn't right now. Well... not for everybody. But, anyway..." He took off the hat, rubbed his fingers through a thick layer of hair, and put the hi-roller back on. Maybe the devil did give him the hat. We stood in silence.

"Where'd you get the hat?" I asked.

death letter blues

"I bought it in Texas. You like it?"

"It's a nice hat."

"I'm no fool," he said with class, "I know where to shop. And on that other thing we were talking about... I got a trick up my sleeve."

What does he mean: I have a trick up my sleeve? Johnny over here isn't really going to try and pull a fast one on the Devil, is he? Messing with the Devil isn't like doing a quick color-change, pass, or double-lift during a card "magic" show to a packed high-school auditorium. The Devil must know about Johnny's ace of spades. "So, what's the trick?" I asked.

"I don't believe in any of that ritualistic shit."

"But you did sell your soul? You aren't fucking with me, are you?"

"Oh No! I am *NOT* fuckin' with you! I sold my *Soul*!" He caught some air; "You can trust me on that."

"You must've made the transaction with someone... or something?"

"For sure! It was crazy. There aren't enough words to tell."

"It's sounds like you believe in that 'ritualistic shit'."

117

"No. I believe that it all just kind of stops. There is no eternity. Like when you're asleep, but you're not aware of anything going on. Like when you have no memory of all that time that passed when you were sleeping. Darkness. Nothing." He paused. "I got something for nothing. It was free."

"But you did get something?"

"Yeah."

"So how can all that shit happen, with the crazy lights and you actually getting something, without you thinking that it might be eternal? You might be a *trickster* but you ain't no *gambler*."

"They were cool experiences but still, it's all going to stop. And nobody can do anything about it. Besides, I practice my art." He tipped his hat and began to pack up for the train. "Maybe I'll see you on the train."

Thoughts of Johnny selling his soul to some creepy, old white guy haunted me for a few moments. It was probably better that we didn't talk anymore. There's no way I'm messing with somebody who's connected all the way to the top of Hell's mafia. Living was bad enough.

By this time, the train was pulling in: a cacophony of whistling steam and screeching train wheels. The whole

death letter blues

mechanism consisted of a series of long, silver tubes attached to the rail with iron disks. There were Amtrak staff hanging out of the cars, making sure that people weren't dangerously close to the vehicle or descending the cars. It seems that we are so preoccupied with safety as a response to our fear of death. The fact remains: we'll die when we die and there isn't much anybody can do about it. We can't eat what we want; we can't smoke what we want; we can't drink what we want. Some free society. We can't avoid the inevitable. How about we just let people encounter their fates without intervention? History creates itself in due course.

elgazzar

death letter blues

My seat was one of a pair in the midst of a spacious cabin. It was a wide, synthetic leather chair with a lever to raise the movable ottoman that popped out from underneath. Each cabin had huge vista windows and generous aisles. The announcement on the PA requested that all passengers find and remain in their seats until the ticket collector came by and validated the stubs. The train began to move. It was a bit surprising that they would begin locomotion before all the tickets had been authenticated. Oh well. I sat patiently. There wasn't much to look at since it was dark. Only slowly passing bulbs in the distance could be seen. The ticket collector eventually came to me and extended his hand. Without any exchange of words, I dropped my ticket into his palm, he looked at it, scanned it, stamped it, handed it back to me, and moved on to the next set of passengers. I wish all transactions with other people were that automated. There is no reason to trade silly, empty words at the risk of either offending or being offended by someone else.

After an hour of slow stop-and-go, the long series of train cars came to halt. Of course, it takes an ungodly amount of time to stop a train, let alone position it correctly. It must have been a stop along the way. The gentle rocking motion and the rhythm of the wheels rolling over the railroad ties made me sleepy. After all, my day did begin with an escape from Ciara's clutches. My eyes couldn't shut so I just tapped along with the rhythm and mentally raced the passing bulbs. The bulbs that were nearer always won in the end, so I would try and spatially identify which bulbs seemed closest and then race them. Usually, I would bet on the dimmer of the two bulbs. Each race cost me a dollar. I kept losing dollars to myself. It was short-lived, but fun, game.

death letter blues

The train came to another stop. A huge billboard boasting the best local variety of barbecue chips dominated the window I was looking through. I just couldn't see past it in any direction. I read the billboard over and over again. I even noticed the rotting on the posts holding up the over sized sign. I was expecting the train to begin motion again after about fifteen minutes. It didn't start back up. People were moving around the cabins, through the cars, and chattering in their seats. My body finally fell into a deep coma after about forty minutes in front of a seventeen-foot cutout of a bag of Jay's Barbecue Chips.

elgazzar

death letter blues

A sudden jerk of the train awoke me after what seemed like an eternity of sleep. I definitely felt refreshed. It may have been the best, dreamless sleep I've had for almost a week. At least six or seven hours had past since I dropped into my snooze. It was dark in the cabin and most of the passengers were still asleep. I looked out the window and to my amazement the giant billboard of Jay's Barbecue Chips with its rotting post was still sprawling over the entire view. No way! There was no fucking way. I jumped up and searched for the first person I could find.

125

Either I was asleep for five minutes or something is seriously wrong because we were in the exact same place I fell asleep in. Which means that we were still only an hour away from Cleveland. I scurried through the rows of sleeping passengers, through cabins, in search of someone who might have a bit more information than me. Finally, the dining car. There was a server standing behind a bar, half asleep, head in hand.

"Excuse me."

"Huh?" The server was actually totally asleep. He looked up with bloodshot eyes, "What can I get for you?"

"What time is it?"

"Oh...," looking at his watch, "It's about 5:30 am."

"Are you sure?" I asked.

"Um... yeah... It's 5:31." So I was asleep for about six hours. This meant that there was another billboard with identical rotting posts and we just happened to pull my seat up next to it or we haven't moved in six hours.

"Where are we?" I asked.

"Man," the server rubbed his puffy eyes and straightened out his horrible uniform, "I think we're still in

death letter blues

Ohio." So we were less than an hour outside Cleveland? It was worse than I thought.

"Is there something wrong with the train?" I asked.

"I guess you didn't hear the PA announcement last night. There's a train ahead of us that got derailed."

"So what now?" I continued in the same fashion.

"We wait."

"Wait? Aren't there any options?"

"Well, we could either back track to Cleveland and go thirty miles past, switch the lines, and then get back here after another engine comes and drags us from the other end of the train; or we could wait until they clean up the mess on the tracks in front and then just go on through. Either way, it's gonna take another three or four hours, so why waste the fuel?"

"I see." Admittedly, I was confused. There wasn't much to do but wait. By this time, I would've already missed my connection in Schenectady. The server pointed me in the direction of the smoking car. Surely, it would be my new home.

When I got down there, several people had already been nesting in the thick fog of cigarette smoke. Despite my smoking habit, I detested small, enclosed spaces packed with numerous smokers. Those tight quarters are made even tighter with carbon-monoxide saturated haze. The only thing that makes the experience of smoking with others in a small space, is when the ventilation system pumps the same smoky air right back into the room. No windows, no exhaust, nothing. On top of all that, the smokers, who are usually enslaved to their own idiosyncrasies, do not encourage intelligent conversation. Like I noted before, all they want to do is talk about the downtrodden experience of smoking. That gets old and boring very quickly. Most of the hard plastic seats were already taken. Of course, the seats were plastic so as not to absorb the stench of stale smoke in the fabric. This bunch of smokers seemed to enjoy wallowing in the stagnant, polluted air. I stood silently in the corner where a slight draft provided much needed fresh air. I indulged in my smoke. At least a person could still smoke on a train even if it was an abhorring affair.

Seven people, including me, were stuffed into the room designed for five. The claustrophobia was starting to set in. My body temperature began to rise; beads of saline rolled down my forehead once they formed and I could feel the coolness of the sweat stains absorbed underneath my armpits. Waves of purple flashes decorated with psychedelic patterns temporarily blinded me. I was in need of a seat but too embarrassed to ask for one. Many of the people I used to know prodded me: they thought I was overdosing on this or that drug but it was a condition I was born with. On top of that, I used to chalk it up to 'bad vibes' coming from the walls of an ancient house. Really, it must've been the result of some prenatal experience that I haven't yet unraveled. Somethings happened to me and I don't know what they are. Unfortunately, those things determined the course of my life and how I would relate to tight spaces. 'Just breathe!' people would often say. But breathing only made it worse. Breathing reminded me of the fact that I was struggling with something and I had to do something to correct it. In short, knowing that something was happening to me made that something worse. The feeling of being too drunk and then smoking some weed, the world spinning inside my head, my stomach gurgling with worry, can only be overcome with calm. Of course, some concerned individual, who never seemed to care before, comes busting down the door asking, "Are you okay? Do you need anything?" And the calm, the composure, the serenity, the peacefulness of victory over the ailment all explode from the depths of my gut. The fuckers who want to talk about everything in order to make themselves feel better always make the nausea worse. So I stepped out between the two cars to get some fresh air.

The sun was now beginning to shine bright through the arched vista windows. People asleep in their seats were beginning to stir. Some were on their way to the restroom, others looked for the dining car for some breakfast. The journey back to my seat resembled a slalom through beautiful women, little kids, old men, and other nondescript, faceless passengers. Conversations were commencing about the miserable state of waiting that we all found ourselves in. Some expressed morbid fears, similar to my fear of flight, on the possibility of this train derailing. Every hour, uninformative and overly vague announcements were made on the PA: "Crews are working hard to clear the wreckage ahead. It'll only be a little while longer before we get going here." The actual facts of the situation remained secret. Of course, the train engineer and conductor knew specifics of the scenario ahead as well as a good estimate as to how long it would take. Reporting to a flustered group of travelers that they are to be imprisoned in immobility for eight hours would result in a flurry of questions and a barrage of insults. The use of the PA was a preemptive attempt at the pacifying the prisoners. Otherwise, a full-scale riot could potentially erupt, not to mention the costly refunds and comps that would ultimately lead to filing Chapter 11 Bankruptcy.

Instead of raising hell, most of the vacationers and commuters happily purchased fare from the dining car. With wide grins, they would return to their seat assignments, unfold the hinged eating trays attached to their armrests, and carefully unpack the tuna-cracker-mayonnaise-brownie novelty items that they paid eight dollars for. What a lucrative swindle! A real monopoly: hungry people cheerfully paying top dollar for bad food because they had no other options. I could go days without eating. Food was never really a passion of mine. Come to think of it, besides hats (my knowledge of which is happenstance, not earned), I don't have any passions. Nothing spawns me into action or anger. Things are generally boring.

More time passed. More tuna was sold. More babies cried. More PA announcements blared. More cigarettes were smoked. More travelers complained. And then finally, the train began to move at a snail's pace and everyone on board erupted in applause.

"Don't get too excited," the PA announced, "we won't be moving much faster than this." The applause and 'yahoos' turned into 'boos' and 'damns'. I was pleased by the simple fact that I would be able to see past the huge billboard. Shit.

Every ten minutes or so, the train would come to another halt, receive an overwhelming disapproval, and then build speed again. The dining car was offering complimentary coffee for the inconvenience of being on the delayed train; it was a small expenditure considering the alternatives. I poured myself a cup and headed down to the smoking room. Only one person was in the closet. A very skinny white guy with a shaved head. He had big, bug eyes and two light eyebrows that hovered above. He seemed sick and weak to me.

"Hey," he said.

"Hey."

"It's nice when there aren't a lot of people in here, huh?" he said in a terribly fast rhythm.

"Yeah... I guess." I agreed since I didn't come down to talk; I came down to smoke.

"Now if we ever get to where we're going, things would be better. I just can't wait to get off this train. There isn't really much to do but socialize and talk to people and that gets really old. Don't you think?"

I just looked at his big, golf-ball sized eyes and the puffy bags underneath.

"Well? Don't you?" he continued, "I mean really, who wants to sit around in a small room talking to people who only want to come down and spend time with you because they want to smoke and end up ignoring you the whole time and then they think you're annoying but don't even really want to say anything about it, ya know?"

I just raised my eyebrows, nodded, took a drag, and thought about run-on sentences. Clearly, this man's meta-cognitive sense was underdeveloped. He didn't realize that he was talking about the very situation he was in. Or maybe he did. I don't know. He may have just had a bad experience: someone came down for a quick smoke, and told him that they weren't interested in his chit-chat.

"I just want to get somewhere," I said, "and smoke. I'm not much for conversations." Just then, an older woman with big, silver curls and a cane entered the smoking lounge.

"Hello," she squeaked.

"Hey," the two of us said in unison

133

"How come you don't want to talk?" the man asked.

"Who? Me?" the woman replied.

"No. Him." He was pointing right at me.

"I'm just not much for conversation. I just want to smoke."

"Then what? Go back to your seat and sit quietly, thinking about your life and all its miseries, hoping that something will come along and save you from it?" He rapped off several words in a row. I needed a few seconds to think about what he said. "What? You're just going to ignore me now?"

"Let him be, Eddy," the older woman said. Apparently they had met previously. She then turned to me and put her little hand on my shoulder, which made me very uncomfortable, and asked, "Do you not feel like talking right now?"

"Nothing's coming to save me," I replied to Eddy's question and then moved away from the old lady's light and soothing gesture, "...or you. We're stuck on this damn train." Turning to the woman I said, "And no, I don't feel like talking." She was done with her Virginia Slim cigarette fairly quickly and left.

death letter blues

"Whatever man," Eddy continued, "I haven't had a decent conversation since being on this train. And fuck it, if nobody wants to talk to me, I'll have to talk to my-damn-self." He pulled out a small vial from his pocket, poured a little powder on to the top of his hand and sniffed it. This explained a lot to me. He looked up, rubbing his nose, holding up the container towards me, "Feel like talking?"

"No," I said, "I still don't feel like talking." He went on and on about how often he partied, about the people he met partying, and how often they partied. Fast Eddy was beginning to annoy me. I hadn't had a proper smoke for a long time. Too long. And he was not helping me enjoy my addiction in the least. He was a coke-addict, not a smoker. He smoked to take the edge off when he couldn't blow. I smoked to take the edge off life. I just wanted to relax with my smoke and he was making it impossible with his pleas for attention, connection, and conversation. I had already put out one unsatisfying butt so I smoked another. He rambled for ten straight minutes after sniffing his powder.

Then, he quieted down. Although, he had an off-tempo techno beat twitch. There was no reason for me to look at him. He didn't say too much and I was beginning to feel like we were going to work it out.

"Where you going anyway?" He asked.

"Can we please just not talk?" And he should know better than to ask.

"I was only asking where you were headed to." Eddy seemed a bit hurt.

"Please! Just stop talking."

"Man... If I feel like talking, I'm talking. If you don't want to talk, you don't have to." But resilient.

"But I want quiet." A fact.

"Then you're going to have to leave." He pointed to the narrow sliding door separating this small smelly space and the rest of the train.

"And when I'm gone, do you talk to yourself?" I gave him a smug chuckle with the absolute brilliance of my witty retort.

"Sometimes... but, hey, we're talking now, aren't we?"

What could be said? Nothing. I was defeated but it was quiet. For a moment, I thought that I would accomplish my goal, that my desires would manifest, that I might become whole. Just kidding.

death letter blues

Why was I still here? Because I wanted to smoke?
Because this was a fierce king-of-the-hill military exercise?
Because of who could get the other guy to leave first? For
a moment I seemed to have forgotten that there was a way
out.

In one motion, the sliding door flung open, a
cigarette butt was deadened on the floor, and I left. Eddy
was still talking to himself in the middle of the stench.
Two people walked past me in the direction of the smoking
room. I smiled to their fates.

elgazzar

death letter blues

Almost twenty hours after leaving Cleveland, we finally arrived in Schenectady. As we disembarked, announcements were made about connecting trains, accommodations, and alternatives. When we got off the train, a small group of Amtrak staff and engineers gathered to form an ad hoc committee to deal with the imminent logistical-problem-solving-nightmare that was about to occur. Surely, the staff must've been hoping that Schenectady was a final destination for most of the passengers. But we were really in the middle of nowhere.

139

elgazzar

This was a small, run-down, time-warp town inhabited by ma-n-pa business owners and a generation of bored adolescents discovering the pleasures of crystal-meth. Not a place I wanted to be very long. The sooner I spoke with the committee, the sooner I could begin my countdown to departure. The group of problem-solvers pointed me in the direction of another group of people; this time, they were gathered because they were all headed to Montréal or other points north.

"Is this the group headed to Montréal?" I asked.

A resounding 'Yup' came from about ten people huddled to discuss their options. Most of them were tired and in need of a bed. One person asked if anybody was interested in taking a shuttle or a van the rest of the way. And still others, just didn't seem to care. Apparently, a critical mass of travelers had to agree to take the van in order to justify the cost of the rental; hence, the conversations. One girl in particular pushed hard to convince others of this option. She was to catch a flight out of Montréal in the morning and waiting until the next train would cause her to miss it. She begged and pleaded with the others; she made arguments about the unreliability of the trains, the people waiting for them at the destinations, the speed at which we would arrive, and even the

140

relationships we could foster. 'We're travelers!' she cried, 'That's what an adventure is!' I could've conceivably ridden with her to our next stop up until she started into the whole relationship thing. On top of that, She oozed traveler's pretension: the glorified idea that traveling is a process that provides some gnostic insight into the secrets of the human spirit and she possessed both the privileged position of being able to travel as well as the earned insight from it. These cool adventurers escape life to the remotest corners of the globe and immerse themselves in the local flavor for a month at a time. Upon return, they claim to understand not only the intricacies of the indigenous culture (and the thousands of years of collective consciousness passed down from generation to generation) but also the encoded and mysterious clue to what universally binds all humanity. They really are funny people and pretentious too.

"So, have you all agreed on how you want to get up there?" the conductor was checking on the progress.

"Well, we're one person short. Will that do?" The traveler girl took on the role of advocate.

"You need six people, minimum. Any less than that and we're just going to pair you all off and put you in hotels until tomorrow morning when the next train comes

141

through." The idea of getting paired off and asked to share a cheap hotel room horrified me. Then again, I didn't have to participate in all this mess. I could just walk away, show up in the morning, and adjust my ticket.

"You!" The girl walked towards me.

"Huh?"

"You! You're coming on the van." She grabbed me from underneath my arm. "Yeah," she continued, "We got six."

"Okay," said the conductor, "Grab all of your belongings. Have the baggage handler validate the stubs for your checked luggage and we'll all meet up out front, curbside. Any questions?"

While several of the people had their concerns addressed, I headed towards the curb. There were about three taxis waiting in a line. They were all mini-vans. Were we going to pile six people into this minivan and drive for six hours? That fucking sucks. The nice thing about driving long distances is the comfortable driver's seat. Besides, if you're driving, you're not bored because you're actually doing something and not just sitting. The rest of the group slowly made their way to the curb and gathered again. They all seemed a little worried at not knowing what exactly was going on. The conductor came out with his clipboard, exchanged words with one of the taxi-drivers for about five minutes, signed some papers, and then signaled to the passengers to get into the van. We all got in and the driver pulled away.

Before long, we were outside of the Schenectady city limits and onto a two-lane highway. It was nice to be back at sixty miles per hour. Every hour, the driver would fiddle with the radio trying to dial into the local public station. Public radio in these parts amounted to news, talk, and obscure music programming. Guests on the station argued about the war, the economy, renewable energy, civil liberties all in an attempt to galvanize the public and move them into one of two distinct, but painfully similar, parties. As long as the two parties disagreed on one issue, a metaphorical wedge was driven between them. The wedge merely represented a nonexistent ideological difference in world-views. If, at any moment, for a reason unknown, a nuclear warhead soars through the atmosphere headed towards any town that I may find myself in, and without warning or delay, a bright flash engulfs all that we see, then this very fact remains: there's no use in worrying. So many issues remained off the table: mega-earth-destroying weapons, legalizing drugs, reforming social security, overhauling the public health-care system, and how corporations ought to be punished for breaking the law. The narrowness in perspectives and homogeneity of thought caused me to not vote. No alternatives were possible. It was a deadlocked system that people were willing to fight over. Not me. No way. I just wanted to get back to my apartment and shut the world out: I wasn't gay, I paid my rent on time, I was healthy, I didn't indulge in illegal drugs much, and my hourly wage working in a kitchen wasn't taxed too heavily. There was nothing for me to care about.

The people in the van had quiet conversations with each other. Some others talked on their cell phones and explained the circumstances they found themselves in. I sat in the back and looked out the window. It was dark when we left so I resumed my distant-bulb-racing-game. It kept me entertained for quite a while.

"How much longer?" One of the passengers asked. Every conversation all of sudden stopped as we all anxiously awaited a favorable response.

"Oh... We got about two hours left," replied the driver.

death letter blues

"Thanks." The conversations started back up. In the best of all possible worlds, I could actually begin my return to futility in three hours. It won't be long.

"So, you think we could stop for a snack or something? Maybe a bathroom break?" One of the passengers asked.

"Yeah. A break sounds good," answered the driver. "We'll get off at the next exit." Only after hearing several of the passengers speak up did I really take note of them. Seven of us, including the driver, were speeding north on the Adirondack Northway, looking for an exit. There was the girl who took it upon herself to organize the van and convince people of why they needed to leave now. Then there was an older woman traveling with a young boy who was asleep most of the time. She combed through the boy's hair with her fingers, melancholic, looking out the window. The driver, well, I couldn't describe him. I only really saw the back of his head; he had dark hair. One man, sitting shotgun, wore a t-shirt and baseball hat. The temperature was cooling so I noticed that he didn't have any other layers on. The last of the passengers was a short, balding man in a gray suit and glasses. He's the one who asked how much longer. He's the one who asked for the potty break.

elgazzar

We pulled into some gas station. I jumped out of the van and went inside. The four or five aisles were lined with typical gas station fare: day-old-rotating hot dogs, coffee that was brewed to look like tea (decaf), coffee that was brewed to look like crude oil (regular), chips, candy bars, etc. I bought some more smokes and lit one up once I got outside. As I smoked, my feet casually waddled me towards the van. The man sitting shotgun, with the t-shirt, approached me.

He gestured with his hands for a cigarette. He was asking without words. I packed in my new box, unwrapped it, and pulled one out for him. He then gestured for the lighter. After he took his first full drag, he turned to me.

"*Sank* You."

"Sure." I nodded to him.

"I don *khave* no *monees* to buy. I sorry." Based solely on his accent, I couldn't tell if he was Russian or Puerto Rican. He was dark though. Ahh, the power of logical-mathematical thinking: he was Puerto Rican.

"It's cool," I said.

"You go Canada?"

"Yes."

death letter blues

"I go too. To see baby and wife. Long time I *don* see *dem*." He paused and then continued to tell me of the last time he saw his family. His broken English proved to be a bit of a challenge but he strung the words along in a coherent way. He left out all the unnecessary adjectives and too-precise verbs that most people think make language worth using; I tend to think that verbosity only clutters simple ideas.

He began to tell me his story, which I never asked to hear. He began with remembering that he had stopped at this very gas station with a carpool headed for Canada. A year and a half had gone by since seeing his baby. And when he got to the border, they pulled him out of the car and told him that he couldn't come into the country. He proved his legal status in the U.S. and even jumped through the hoops of getting a visa to enter Canada since he wasn't technically an American Citizen. They told him that he didn't have enough money to come through the border. He had only forty-four dollars the last time. That wasn't enough to get into Quebec. He argued with them for an hour, he said. He even appealed to their sense of humanity: all he wanted was to see his wife and child, who lived in Canada. They refused. They pointed towards the U.S. side of the border and then left him there. He walked back to an uproarious American side, custom officers hollering about how they hated their jobs and hated their Canadian counterparts even more. They exchanged stories of how they would refuse entry to some "shady" Canadian characters based on arbitrary and personal reasons. They resented the Canadians and particularly the quebecois. Despite the United States' economic largesse, to these working people on the border, the quebecois were a real strain of bourgeoisie. Being dominant was just as much a cultural superiority as it was economic; the boys working the gate were completely familiar with the Canadian arrogance: the we've-got-our-shit-figured-out-and-we're-culturally-more-civilized-than-the-most-accoutered-Americans chip on the shoulder. So they just left the poor Puerto Rican man to his own devises on the border with forty-four dollars in his pocket. He ended up meeting another young guy, also brown, who was also refused entry into Canada and was equally broke. He continued to tell me that while it was not was he desired, the challenge of trusting and depending on somebody he didn't know for the sake of solving their predicament was an enlightening experience that he would have never sacrificed. He also felt that he built a relationship with the other fellow in the spirit of solidarity as they camped out on a lake for four days trying to figure out their next move. Eventually, they made it back to their respective points of origin hitchhiking, scrounging meals, and walking. It was incredible that they were able to take of each other even though they didn't know one another. To him, this was what life was all about: when life becomes bleak and despair sets in, the utter hopelessness demands much needed relationships and through those connections, the person begins to believe that only one of two scenarios are viable solutions: success or suicide. He argued that in most cases, people will exceed the challenge of living by creating victory out of virtually nothing. I could take it or leave. Either way it was a nice story.

"My name *i* Wilfredo." He offered his hand.

Nobody had returned to the vehicle. Everyone was standing around socializing. The driver was nowhere in sight. Wilfredo was smoking his cigarette and looking around in nostalgia.

"Come *wi* me," he said.

"Where to?" I asked.

"*Jost* come *wi* me." He walked towards the back of the gas station and headed into some bushes. Of course, I couldn't help but just go along, occasionally checking over my shoulder to make sure that we weren't being left behind. We walked on a trail for about two minutes. Wilfredo stopped.

"Look," he said, pointing ahead to a steep drop. We were standing on one side of a high ravine. Seeing that I was no geologist (or whatever), it could've been a small canyon. Looking down, there was a sheer face; almost a one-hundred and fifty foot drop. Now and then, I could make out some shimmering from the surface of the rushing water below. It was easier to hear the water than to see it.

"You like *i*?" Wilfredo asked.

"Yeah. Sure. It's cool." We stood in silence for a moment listening to the flowing water. "We should get back," I said as we turned towards the van. He followed me back up the trail. Hiking at night can be a somewhat disorienting experience: trails don't seem familiar and my astronomical navigation skills haven't been honed. We popped out of the trees from the opposite side of the gas station. We definitely didn't return the same way. As we made our way around the corner, the vehicle was gone. Fuck!

"Fuck!"

death letter blues

"Man, no worry, man." Wilfredo tried to calm me. But seeing that this was all his idea, I didn't want to hear him speak at all.

"Now what? You want to walk to Canada?"

"*Is* no *prowlem,* man."

"Yes! It is a problem. Who is going to come by and pick us up from here? I don't even know where we are!" If Wilfredo didn't know that I was raging by the tone of my voice and words coming out of my mouth, then he must've understood from body language: arms waving hysterically in the air, pacing back and forth, and at least three cigarettes smoked. People tend to think that foreigners with accents are stupid because they aren't privy to the latest trends in slang and feel that they often have to either slow down their speech or repeat themselves. I happen to believe that Wilfredo over here knew exactly how I felt despite his linguistic handicap. In fact, I was getting the feeling that he was trying to teach me a lesson by modeling composure under duress. This could've been an intentional act on his part to emulate the dreamy romance he felt the last time he was in a spot of bother. This was no story to be told and retold. I just want to deliver this fucking letter to the rightful owner, get back to my apartment and be done with this whole thing. So far, nothing has gone well for me. Shit, even if it was going well, I wouldn't know the difference; this all sucks. I should never have agreed to any of this. I could've taken GiGi's money, gone to a shrink about my fear of flight, and been back the same fucking day. Instead, I get wise old Wilfredo, who's trying to teach me some lesson about a life I'm not interested in. In a perfect world, which doesn't exist (unless, of course, you're interested in misery), the protagonist, personified in this case by me, would learn some deep lesson about human nature and make changes in behavior based upon those epiphanies. After all, it isn't the pit of despair and the escape from pain that causes people to learn, it's the victories, however small, that remind us of the fortitude and perseverance that the average Joe is capable of exhibiting once begun on a track of winning. Unfortunately, this is not happening for me.

I stormed off in the direction of the woods. There was something about the sound of rushing water that I instinctually desired. There, at the precipice overlooking the small canyon, I stood. The rustling of the leaves nearby alerted me. It was only Wilfredo.

"I sorry, man, about *dis*."

death letter blues

No words came from my mouth. The distant sounds of the stream filled my head. And already, I had forgotten the whole affair. I wanted to get back, but I couldn't understand why I was angry. It just happened to me. But it was gone now.

"Hey, man, I sorry about *dis*."

"Huh? Yeah. Okay. Forget it."

"But is nice here, no?"

"It's calm."

Wilfredo was a short man. The top of his head was level with my shoulder. He was skinny too. He wore baggy t-shirts and baggy jeans to conceal his frailty. He stood next to me on the cliff. From the corner of my eye, I could tell that Wilfredo turned to me. His mouth was moving. He was saying something. Only the sound of the rapids beneath filled my head. The white noise from the bottom of the ravine dominated all of my senses. It became overwhelming. I was looking at him, but there was not even a semblance of an attempt on my part to make out what he was saying. The uproar of the raging stream reached a crescendo and my arms, outstretched, had just hurled little Wilfredo over the edge.

elgazzar

For several moments, my body remained fixed, filled with the very waves that flooded my ears, looking down into the canyon. Nothing moved. Only that sound. A short chuckle materialized from the shallowest parts of my gut and I walked off the cliff. As I sank through the air, I realized that this was not a curious instant for what might come after nor was this a departure from a desperate and cruel world. It was a stroll. For a moment, I had even begun to believe that I was flying. But I wasn't flying; I was falling. A truly peaceful moment. A moment that lasted an eternity. It was during this passing second of dream-time consciousness that I was aware for the first and last time of the approaching fate I was always designed to achieve. Just like a hammer's sole purpose is to beat nails, so this was mine. It was a long time coming. It was inevitable. The bottom of the canyon was approaching and a qualm full of fear and regret gripped me. Perhaps in the morning, a young boy hiking in delight would come across two corpses mutilated by the thrashing of water and rock. The authorities would not be able to explain the motives behind this improbable act. The investigators would creatively name it for reporters in the spirit of inexplicability: a cult suicide. This was not suicide. And that is what scared me most; I didn't know what it was either. A stroll off an escarpment driven by impulse and my own futility in face of myself, the consequences of which I was not willing to accept. The opacity of the black, shimmering surface of water would soon make me painfully aware of its dynamic nature, both fluid and firm. And if that flash of stinging torture does not, then surely the sharp rocks beneath the surface will. The fear. To hell with fucking Montréal. To hell with the letter and GiGi and my mother and Wilfredo. Those people had propelled me to this.

My mind was still churning after my body was dead. It circled round and round on things I missed: retelling stories I've already lived. My body lay in the river. The rags of shredded material flagging on the waves of the rapids. Nothing.

elgazzar

death letter blues

A burst of beaming sunlight shot onto my face and I squinted. My body shuffled. My bladder was throbbing. My eyes opened and after the initial rush of illumination, the contrast of objects far and near began to settle into something perceptible. My body flung to a seated position and I looked around disoriented and confused. I was in my apartment on my couch. Something inside of me cried in terror as I attempted to piece together this occurrence. After pissing, I sat back on the couch. I lit a cigarette. A fucking dream? What? My butt itched. The letter? GiGi? Ciara? Wilfredo? The cliff? All a dream?

The phone rang. Unusual.

"Hello?"

"Ruiz? Ruiz, Bernard?" the woman's voice on the other end inquired.

"Who's speaking?" I needed information before I answered any questions.

"This is your Auntie GiGi," the voice announced, expecting some sort of reciprocal excitement.

"Who?"

The conversation seemed awkwardly familiar, but that was all a dream. Deja vu, I guess. The woman on the other end claimed to be some long lost friend of my dead mother who entrusted her with secrets for safekeeping and wanted me, the good son, to travel across the continent in order to deliver some letter, the contents of which are unknown, to some address that may or may not exist. She asserted to be too old for the journey herself and a younger, intelligent, able-bodied, more caring son would be more fitting for the task. She offered a generous sum of money for the trek and looked to have a serious interest in my success.   All I wanted to know was what the letter contained.

"I don't know," she said, "It's sealed."

"Hmm."

"Well will you go?" she asked.

"Huh? Yeah. Sure. I'll go."

THE END

www.ingramcontent.com/pod-product-compliance
Lightning Source LLC
Chambersburg PA
CBHW020620250626
47154CB00004B/1598